About the Author

Brenda Anderson is a new author. She was raised in Kaysville, Utah, U.S.A., and has taught English and has been a school librarian in various places in the U.S.A. and the U.A.E.

The Epictetus Dilemma

Brenda Anderson

The Epictetus Dilemma

Olympia Publishers
London

www.olympiapublishers.com
OLYMPIA PAPERBACK EDITION

Copyright © Brenda Anderson 2023

The right of Brenda Anderson to be identified as author of this work has been asserted in accordance with sections 77 and 78 of the Copyright, Designs and Patents Act 1988.

All Rights Reserved

No reproduction, copy or transmission of this publication may be made without written permission. No paragraph of this publication may be reproduced, copied or transmitted save with the written permission of the publisher, or in accordance with the provisions of the Copyright Act 1956 (as amended).

Any person who commits any unauthorised act in relation to this publication may be liable to criminal prosecution and civil claims for damage.

A CIP catalogue record for this title is available from the British Library.

ISBN: 978-1-80074-870-5

This is a work of fiction. Names, characters and incidents originate from the writer's imagination. Any resemblance to actual persons, living or dead, is purely coincidental. Any existing locations are fictionalized.

First Published in 2023

Olympia Publishers
Tallis House
2 Tallis Street
London
EC4Y 0AB

Printed in Great Britain

Chapter One
Carlos Diaz

Men are disturbed not by things, but by the views which they take of things. Thus, death is nothing terrible, else it would have appeared so to Socrates. But the terror consists in our notion of death, that it is terrible.

Epictetus, *The Enchiridion* as translated by Thomas Wentworth Higginson as found in The Gutenberg Project.

Some say death tastes like peppermint. My name is Elle Magellan, and I'm a historian for an organization called The Plato Foundation. I watch the actions of one part of our secret society. Everything. And then I write what I see. I have digital recordings: I don't have to remember everything I document. I mostly document death.

How do I see? Cameras – legal and not. Seer stones – "magical" stones seers use to see forward and backward in time, to discern thought, and to ask other questions about the present. The most powerful stones are harnessed by technology, meaning a magician has to be viewing a screen otherwise blank to an observer to see the full scene being watched, but the stone's results are projected from a dark space to a screen and can be seen by initiated magicians. I work in a black magic society. There are white magic societies, but their ways are not our ways. Magicians must be initiated into our black magic society to be able to see our magical screens.

These more powerful seer stones are useful for documenting areas where we cannot access cameras or sound. There are less powerful seer stones, but those will be discussed later in the history.

I'm considered a seer in our world. Can I know others' thoughts? Some say I do. I use "the lights" as seer stones are sometimes called by us. In my history which I am writing now much like Nick Carraway in *The Great Gatsby*, I will sometimes share a person's thoughts. The "lights" are useful for this.

I am narrating for the sake of our foundation's records. I tell rather than show a lot. Telling is considered a writing sin by some, but I'll try to accommodate with dialogue and description when I feel like it serves the purpose of the historical account. I'll touch base throughout. In our game – the game of deaths – everything is seen by someone. I'm that someone for a few numbered players and kings.

"This really may be the endgame," Carlos has said about this year. No one knows what this means.

"I've got your number" is a true threat in our world. It means someone has your death number and implies their death number is higher than yours which means your final life is in their hands if in a you are not protected by the game to die and survive. . Satan, Carlos Diaz as he is currently called, is useful for a bit of information it turns out. And – fun fact – the devil looks a bit like a youngish Yul Brynner with better hair than Brynner ever had. Cats have nine lives. Humans have one life most people believe. There are ways to die more than once and live. And the more one dies and lives through it, the better one lives, if that makes paradoxical sense: fame, glory, wealth, beauty, and more are yours as your deaths increase. And if one lives six hundred and sixty-six times and doesn't die, one might be immortal. That's the theory amongst the cohorts. Carlos Diaz, Satan, or the devil, as he is all called, isn't saying yet what the endgame is. A new game is coming. The current game – The Epictetus Dilemma – is still afoot tonight, twenty-seven December 2028; it should have ended Christmas Eve at midnight. Unprecedented.

Why are we willing to die? Satan states death is scientifically demanded for power and wealth to exist. He calls it counter-balancing, and I get it to an extent. We, in the black magic secret societies all over the world have become quite civilized in this age. We die ourselves rather than innocents dying to pay the death quotas.

Right now, I'm listening to "Whatever It Takes" by Imagine Dragons. Fits our society. Members tend to crave the adrenaline which come with living to die.

Chapter Two
Cemetery

Let me, Elle Magellan, start near the end of my story with an incident involving some professors from the law school at Minnesota's University of St. Thomas.

James Madison, Franklin Washington, and Oscar Fouad stood in the darkness, a few minutes just after midnight on Christmas Eve 2028 looking at the upturned graves in a Jewish cemetery near Minneapolis. African-American Franklin Washington crouched with his 5'8" muscular body near the snow and picked up some frozen dirt clumps. Franklin Washington was fifty-five and well-loved at the law school, in Minnesota, and elsewhere in the United States. Washington was planning on soon running for the U.S. Senate.

"A local cemetery owner sold this part of the cemetery to billionaire Al Thatch. The graves are all over a hundred years old and have few relatives around to protest. Still. Feels spiritually dangerous," Franklin Washington explained as he chewed on the toothpick in his mouth.

Madison and Fouad both shifted in their tan wool coats, all three dressed in full suits and ties beneath their winter wool dress. All had intended to attend St. Thomas School of Law's midnight Christmas mass but had wandered off as the cheerful crowd increased.

"Let's just go over there and look at the damage as it has

been suggested the cemetery was in play during the game—that the dug-up graves contributed to the Osiris Foundation's lead," Madison had suggested. The cemetery had been a thirty-minute drive away in the surprisingly warm night for December in Minneapolis on 72 Street and Penn Avenue. A storm was coming creating a cloud cover.

Madison now quietly laughed at Franklin's comment as he looked at the rocks on top of the nearby tombstone. James Madison was thirty-five, fit, blonde, and sarcastically kind. "You superstitious, Washington?"

"Not going to say I'm not. Digging up the dead – especially notably old dead – isn't sport, friend, as you remember from our Las Vegas trip." Washington quietly laughed. "I wouldn't have done this. Yes. A bit superstitious."

A loud flutter of wings pushed its way through the air. "Damn." Fouad turned. Thirty-five-year-old Egyptian Oscar Fouad was also handsome and Madison's best friend. Washington stood up and looked with Madison in time to see a great blue heron fly out across the dug-up graves into the winter night.

Madison shivered. Washington corrected Fouad, "Don't curse in a cemetery."

Madison laughed.

Fouad responded, "Seriously, Washington, you are making me feel like a Dickens ghost is going to come around a tomb. Let's get out of here."

"Come on, Franklin." Madison lightly tugged on Washington's coat. Washington stood up.

Franklin Washington and Oscar Fouad first descended the mound of frozen dirt and snow the men had been standing on to survey the taped off area. James Madison stood there for a bit and said, "This is not going to end well. But this has not been in play in the past few months. The graves have just recently been exhumed. I don't understand the dead, it appears."

Chapter Three
The Epictetus Dilemma

"Do you believe Holy Guardian Angels sleep?" Washington trudged through the snow toward St. Thomas School of Law two nights later, December 26, 2028. The blackout of the buildings in all of the area had resulted from the fierce snowfall that had come down earlier in the afternoon. It was early in the evening dark, and the snow had stopped leaving mounds of unplowed white everywhere. Christmas break was in full swing, but the men had come to St. Thomas earlier in the night at the Minneapolis campus near the Target building to discuss the conclusion of The Epictetus Dilemma.

Fouad responded, "Not."

"Hm," Richard Emerson, a white-haired, seventy-two-year-old professor who had joined the group, said.

"I think they must not. They're always at hand," Madison commented as all four men stopped as Fouad stumbled over a mound covered in snow.

"Holy shit. This is a dead body," Fouad responded. All of the men walked over to the site.

"Sure enough," Washington whispered.

"Shit," Emerson said. "I don't have time for this crap."

Madison quietly laughed. "Wait. He's breathing. And bleeding."

"Damn it," Emerson swore again.

"He'll die out here," Washington commented. "It's -15 degrees."

"Hell no," Madison said. "We are not moving this guy anywhere."

"We are." Washington positioned himself on the right side of the man's torso. "Lift him with me."

"We are going to end up on the news tomorrow," Emerson said. "I don't like this, Franklin. Let's call 911 – I see Fouad already is – and leave him here until they come."

"We don't know how long he's been here. He could die out here." Franklin Washington sighed. "Pick him up."

All of the men picked him up and as best they could – for he was a large man – carried him into the building's foyer – a building four stories high with a glass wall the height of the building. The man had been shot. It was dark in the blackened-out building save for the cold moon shining into it. They had keys. It was holiday break and no one was there they supposed. All of the men stood in the dark looking at the wounded man lying on the ground. A trail of blood from the man's left shoulder had strung through the snow and into the law school on the marble floor. The wounded man now looked dead.

The men turned as the sound of shouting came from stories above. Washington took off his coat and placed it over the man to warm him. If alive. Who knew at this point? He now didn't look like he was breathing. Fouad started CPR.

"What in the hell are you guys doing?" Cotton Anderson, the dean of the law school, was seemingly taking two steps at a time down every flight of stairs and cursing words worse than, and including, "f—ing pains in my arse" at the men he loved below him.

"Good Lord, you guys, this is the worst idea ever." Cotton

Anderson could not run fast enough.

Madison pointed at Washington.

"Who is he?" Anderson thundered as he rounded the final staircase and stomped across in the dark to where the men stood and the body lay near the front doors of the school's entrance. "Who killed him?" Anderson was still shouting. "I'm not kidding. Whom do we have to cover for tonight?"

"It wasn't any of us," Washington stated. "He would have been found dead outside the law school in the morning if we would have left him. It's Eventide (our term for the night after the game ends each year) this twenty-sixth of December – the game is over. I know you know, Cotton. We can't have the police finding a body in the morning. We found it outside. Protocol is that we save him if needed, if our knowledge base about the victim is zero."

"He looks completely dead already!" Cotton roared in the dark.

"He wasn't dead when we picked him up. Maybe we killed him." Madison smiled as he took out a cigarette from his coat.

"Always helpful." Fouad smiled at Madison, and Madison returned the friendly understanding. Fouad continued CPR. Death was not strange to these men. Their light-hearted demeanor was a coping mechanism.

"Put away the cigarette!" Cotton Anderson sort of comically swiped at Madison's arm. Cotton Anderson was a head shorter than all of the men who were between 5'10" and 6'2". At 5'5", Anderson could still scare the crap out of any grown-up including these two young men, Madison and Fouad. Washington and Emerson were Anderson's peers so did not fear him as much, but time meant money in their dangerous

15

game, The Epictetus Dilemma, and Cotton was the keeper of time, money, life, and more in this game for these guys. He could kill and not think twice and no one would find out. Still, these four men were his own. Cotton wanted answers.

"I'm not kidding." This time, Cotton Anderson's voice was soft and dangerous. "If I later find out any of you had a hit out on this guy and the player did it in front of the law school to let you know the job was done, I'm going to f— you up before I forgive any of you."

"Clear," Washington said. A green light appeared on Washington's Omega watch.

"Clear," Emerson said. Green.

"Clear," Madison said. Green.

"Clear," Fouad said. Green.

Cotton Anderson was not wearing a watch.

"Thank God," Anderson replied. Red and blue lights appeared in the street. Men came through the snow with a stretcher. The men in the law school could see their shapes approaching in the darkness.

Madison pointed out a small tattoo – an 808 – on the deceased's wrist, but it looked like two infinity signs with an opal between. "He's with us?"

"Not sure what's going on here, Cotton," Washington responded.

The men stood in silence. The police, firemen, and paramedics were approaching.

"Wait," Cotton Anderson said. "I had him killed. I forgot."

All of the men looked over at Cotton.

Pounding on the door resulted in Oscar Fouad and James Madison opening the doors to the paramedics who soon declared the man dead and took the body away. Madison had an unlit cigarette hanging between his teeth.

"We'll clean," Cotton Anderson responded as the men asked him some questions about the situation and if they needed help cleaning up the blood that had trailed behind the body. Some of these police and firemen had a clear notion St. Thomas School of Law housed the most dangerous game and had a clearing company on hand for just this sort of thing.

"Poor janitorial staff," the police officer laughed as he closed the door behind him – the last official to leave.

"Yes, poor janitorial staff, Cotton," Emerson was now yelling. "You dueled us, Cotton. Pay us. You scared the shit out of me asking me to declare myself clear, Anderson. Explain yourself. Your number is higher than ours, we're on the ground, I can't tell if the game is on, and I am under you, so you could have literally taken us out. "

"For my mistake, US$10,000 is already in each of your accounts." Cotton Anderson headed toward the elevators. "Follow me. I have a lot going on right now, and I can't afford to have anyone beneath me doing deals without letting me know. It's worth a mere forty thousand to see who is still clear. Shit. I can't believe my player killed him in the front yard. Good God. Sorry, Emerson. You know this as well as I do: a game is a game."

"Cotton, the game was supposed to end two nights ago, Christmas Eve, 2028 – the scrolls all said it." Fouad implied his question.

Washington's countenance darkened. "Do you mean to tell me the game is still on the ground?"

All five men were crammed into the elevator now. It was silent inside save for a version of a Beatles song being covered by a modern singer.

Ding.

"Yes." Cotton sighed. "But you know I love it."

"What in the hell happened?" Emerson managed to quietly yell. "Why is the game still afoot? My God, what if that body is traced back to you, Cotton? It was in the snow outside the law school. We'll lose if this goes public."

"It won't linked to me," Cotton assured Emerson.

"It might be linked to someone here. The body was *shot*."

"I know the police chief. He's with us. It won't get to that because it was me. If it would have been any of you, it could have come to the news. It won't. I thought maybe you knew the game was still on." Cotton Anderson opened his office's secretary's space. They all walked in in the dark. The lights sputtered and then went on as electricity returned to the city on twenty-six December 2028.

Beaming light filled the foyer. The blood on the floor was already being cleaned by men in what appeared to be janitorial outfits. Madison smiled to himself. He had complete faith in this system.

The phone in Anderson's office rang. All of the men entered as Cotton picked up the phone. "Yes?" Laughter. "Yes. It was unfortunate that a victim nearby, was hurt and walked here, don't you agree, Chief?" Cotton looked down. "I'm here working on The Epictetus Dilemma. I would hate for this to be in the papers." Madison took a seat. "Great. I'm glad to hear it." Anderson slammed the landline down. He picked up his cell phone, sent a text after writing, "Now kill the killer and blame him."

Chapter Four
Gabrielle (Elle) Magellan

This is Elle. My full name is Gabrielle Magellan. Still here telling the story. Carlos Diaz just contacted me. He insists this history is important. I'm now shifting gears to some of the students of these professors.

Chapter Five
St. Thomas School of Law
Minneapolis Orientation

Earlier that fall, during the start of school at St. Thomas School of Law in the 2028–2029 school year, Winter Thompson sat at her assigned table in the rather large entryway of St. Thomas School of Law on orientation day. She had been a talented and celebrated high school English teacher in a school ranked in the top 5% of high schools in the country by *Newsweek*. Winter desired to become a school district's attorney. She had plans to eventually become a judge of some sort, perhaps in juvenile justice. She looked forward to law school.

A twenty-nine-year-old student named Julia Saunders sat next to Winter, each of whose place tags said their full name and where they were from. Julia whispered, "I've been assigned, Utah, to look out for you since you are a disaffected Mormon in a Catholic law school arena and may not know all of the cultural ins and outs. How do you feel that you've already been discussed and sort of 'handled'? I'm Julia. Julia Saunders."

"I've been handled before. I had my records removed from The Church of Jesus Christ of Latter-Day Saints. Most people know them as Mormons, but they no longer use that name. It's easier for me to call my culture Mormon. I'm somewhat opinionated. The Mormons handled me in that situation. I'll live. I'm Winter Thompson from Salt Lake City, Utah."

"I'm from Chicago, Illinois." Julia smiled. "And I like Mormons."

"I do too. I'm sort of still a cultural Mormon while not being a Mormon."

"Ah." Julia smiled again.

The orientation began. Sitting at their table was a young attractive professor with a card labeling him as Professor Fouad. Julia moved in without shame, flirting openly with her body language, "Professor Fouad, do we need to fully pay attention or just sort of say we've attended?"

"Fully pay attention, of course." Young Professor Oscar Fouad was unphased and a bit amused.

"Of course."

"Ms. Saunders – I see your name is – one must truly listen. Law school isn't only a game."

"That's not true, Professor." Julia smiled.

Winter looked confused. She didn't like how Julia addressed the professor without him introducing himself to them first. They weren't his peers. The flirting was embarrassing. Also at the table were two twenty-something guys: Irish-accented Pete Johnson from Jackson Hole, Wyoming (I can't yet explain the accent), USA, and Khalifa Abdul Mohamed from Abu Dhabi, Abu Dhabi, UAE. Winter wondered why undergrad schools were not listed instead. In addition to a bachelor's from a state school, Winter also had a M.Ed. in education from Brigham Young University; perhaps St. Thomas didn't wish to list everyone's entire CV on their nameplate.

Twenty-three-year-old Pete looked up at Winter who

smiled in return. Dark hair. Darker eyes. He was not redheaded but dark-haired Irish. I, Elle, have wondered what he was doing being raised in Montana. The "lights" say Pete's accent has to do with being raised in Ireland until age ten. Pete smirked and slightly rolled his eyes and looked back at the podium where the dean of the law school, Dean Cotton Anderson, was introducing himself.

" 'To believe your own thought, to believe that what is true for you in your private heart is true for all men, — that is genius. Speak your latent conviction, and it shall be the universal sense; for the inmost in due time becomes the outmost, – and our first thought is rendered back to us by the trumpets of the Last Judgment.' Ralph Waldo Emerson," Cotton Anderson waxed sentimental, "teaches all young readers – lawyers in our case – to trust themselves in his revered essay 'Self-Reliance'."

Julia rolled her eyes. "Good God, this is going to be a long day."

Winter couldn't help but laugh. "I agree, but seriously, you are going to make us targets as troublemakers," she whispered. "Try and hold it together, Julia."

Two hours later, the food came. After lunch, they were to enter the moot courtroom for more instruction with their group as assigned by tables. Meanwhile, Professor Fouad turned and introduced himself to the table. He addressed Winter first, "They are about to serve coffee? Is it forbidden for you?"

"No. I'm no longer Mormon, although I adhere to many of the theologies still."

"I see. Then I will have a coffee cup brought to you. You are missing one in an effort to help you feel as though we were sympathetic to your needs. That's great. Hold on." Oscar

Fouad flagged a waiter and explained. The waiter wandered off in a sort of lost fashion.

Julia commented, "I doubt you'll get coffee during the meal. That guy seemed a bit daft." She laughed and sipped her water.

Winter couldn't decide if she liked Julia. Julia was a little unhinged socially in high stakes settings, Winter felt. But maybe this setting wasn't stressful to Pete and Julia, both of whom went to St. Thomas in undergrad, it turned out. Or to Khalifa Abdul Mohammed who had attended Notre Dame for undergrad – his father had a friend who had a house in South Bend with connections to the school. "Islamic," he told the table as Julia then asked everyone their religious affiliations, and Khalifa was soft-spoken albeit with a strong presence. Khalifa ignored Julia and Winter completely after his religious declaration. He did talk a few times to Pete and Professor Fouad. Everyone else at the table was Catholic.

As they ate, Julia leaned in. "I have an invitation for you from someone you don't know but who is my friend. Want to attend a party with me this weekend?"

"Sure," Winter said. *A party sounded good.* She was no spring chicken at twenty-eight in Mormonland. Most of her undergrad classmates married during undergrad. She had not socialized much since she was about twenty-five simply because all of her friends were married. "Sure," Winter said again, a little more upbeat this time. "That sounds great."

In a beige pencil skirt and a crew neck green sweater with beige heels, Winter's red hair was swept up in a ponytail behind her. She strongly contrasted Julia's almost black hair and extremely tiny frame. Winter weighed about one hundred and thirty, and she could tell little Julia was barely over one hundred. Julia's black hair was sweeping around her shoulders in a flirtatious movement at all times. But she was smart. Winter could tell. Wicked smart. And with a drive to hurt on occasion. Julia was not a force to underestimate. Winter was what some people termed telepathic. Winter termed it observant of the little details that often told a person's whole story.

Winter had an IQ of 179. She kept it secret. She dumbed herself down. She purposefully missed questions on tests, or worse, would see that the test was poorly written and answer accordingly, lowering her score. But she had been courted by MENSA when in elementary when her test scores were so shocking, and her mother and father sat her down and told her what Winter later realized was really good advice: "You are very smart, Winter," her mother had said. "And we love you very much. You need to not tell your friends about the IQ tests and other things. They would not understand. Let's just have fun at school, okay?"

Winter had been popular at the lowest rungs in the highest popularity groups in high school. She was in debate in high school and had average-to-sometimes-excellent grades. No one understood her real abilities and that she met with a MENSA counselor twice a month her entire school years. The MENSA counselor had guided her through various activities and had her participate in think tanks throughout her life. No one at school knew. She loved these days with the MENSA counselor. Winter comprehended at a young age that there were people whom she did not know who knew who she was intelligence-wise, and that they were watching her grow intellectually to see what she could accomplish. It was decided by a team of six people including her MENSA counselor that she would apply to St. Thomas School of Law after teaching for six years. Teaching had taught her how to publicly speak; she had been incredibly shy in high school, albeit friendly and fun.

"Here's my contact information." Winter wrote it on a Post-it note from her red purse and handed it to Julia.

Chapter Six
"Welcome to the Game"

Julia did not knock on Winter's door Friday night. It was Pete. He was not in a good mood. *Delightful*, thought Winter.

"Where's Julia?" Winter asked when Pete greeted her outside her apartment in Bloomington, Minnesota.

"I'm your ride. Julia sent me." *Winter decided she trusted the law school's vetting of people and invited him in to her warm, cozy apartment which smelled like cinnamon,* Pete thought.

"Come in. I'm not quite ready." Winter backed up from the door, giving passage to Pete who entered and looked around. A rose-colored brocade couch from the 1960s was charmingly graced by an oversized leather ottoman covered with a sheep's skin and light gray wool blanket. A very small TV with a DVD player sat next to a baby-blue vinyl record player. One could see into the back bedroom where a queen-sized bed was covered with a salsa-red embroidered bedspread. Books filled the shelves built into the wall. Winter had had to mail her books because they took so much space in her RAV4, space which she needed for her living items when she moved here. Winter stepped into the bathroom and closed the door. When she returned, she had on the exact same makeup but was wearing a pair of jeans, a silver shirt, and a pair of heels.

"Change," Pete demanded.

"Sorry?"

"Change. The shoes. The shirt. Tennis shoes and a sweatshirt. Do it now."

"Pardon?"

"Do what I say."

Winter confusedly went into her bedroom. Pete followed her. He pushed past her and opened her closet. He withdrew a pink sweatshirt (it was the only one she had) and grabbed a pair of Nikes. "Socks?" he asked.

Winter went to the dresser and found a pair of white ankle socks.

"Change."

For some reason, she did. But she followed up with, "I'm not sure I'm up for a party tonight."

Pete responded, "That's what I'd prefer actually."

"Look," Winter finally snapped, "I like Julia. Julia invited me. Where is Julia? Why are you here being rude and demanding I look like a high schooler?"

"The 'party' requires more *athletic* wear, let's just say. You can join Julia when we get there. I'd love nothing more than for you to refuse to come." Pete said nothing else. He was dead silent.

A timer went off on Pete's watch. Pete looked thunderous. "Time's up. You didn't reject the offer. You're coming."

"What?"

"You're coming."

"I'd like to stay here."

Pete reached inside his jacket and pulled a pistol.

"You're coming now. You waited too long to rescind. You aren't cut out for this, but you're doing it. I'm a good read.

You're too timid in my opinion. And you're out of shape. Science shows us through generations that a lack of a response is an affirmative response. I'm required to say this: Welcome to the game. I've been a member of the game for three years. We need to now go get in the car. I will shoot and kill you if you do not, and no one will arrest me."

This is Elle, the narrator. Pete Johnson was at the most difficult point in his participation in the great conversations of the foundations of the star network known as Diaz-United States. He would have actually killed Winter and she would have died squared as it is called by us, and she would have died with no chance of recovery and our foundation would have covered him. He was commanded to act as such. Once a person has been tapped, they participate or die for the safety of the group.

Winter was not reckless enough to question Pete, but she grabbed her purse in an attempt to take her phone with her.

"Leave it. And your phone if it's not in the purse."

Winter threw her purse back on the bed. She walked in front of Pete who grabbed her close and hid the gun in his inner jacket pocket. It was eight September 2028.

Pete practically threw Winter into the passenger side of his black BMW SUV. Winter was considering her options. This might be it. She may lose her life tonight. Pete started the car and locked her in. "Seat belt," he said.

"Are you kidding?" Winter found her voice. "You're worried I might get hurt in a car accident?"

"You heard me. Right now, you are a commodity to me."

"What game? Where is Julia?"

"I will say little, if anything at all, past this point until we see if you live."

First, as soon as the car stopped, Winter would punch and punch Pete and scream once allowed outside of the car, if that ever transpired. She was allowing herself to be taken to a second location, which happened only because she was in shock all the way to the car. She had reasoned there was no way Pete would actually shoot her as they both were in the same cohort at law school. *How had she allowed herself to being taken to a second location?* Winter wondered.

Pete was silent.

Twenty minutes into the drive, Pete turned onto a back street on the outskirts of Minneapolis and she could discern in the dark that they were driving in an industrial warehouse area. *This was bad*, Winter thought. *Bad.*

Pete pulled into an empty parking lot near an unlit building and with a west-facing door propped open in the night with a door stop.

"Get out. Go in that door. You'll understand more as you enter."

"No."

"Get out." Pete pulled the gun. Why she had not followed her plan, she was unsure. Somehow getting out seemed far more dangerous than staying in the car. Pete shuffled the gun – we in my secret world refer to loading a gun as shuffling it – and Winter got out of the car.

Pete drove away. Julia appeared in the open door. She was crying.

Chapter Seven
In the Manner of Skull and Bones

Winter ran toward Julia. "Julia, help me. Pete is dangerous."

"Winter, Pete is with me. I have known we were to be initiated into a fraternity tonight. I had no idea it would be this scary. You are in for good. There is no going back." Julia had tears streaming down her face. Winter turned to run the other way, but she was met by Khalifa who turned her around with a pistol. Khalifa was not smiling.

Even just outside the door, one could smell the strong scent of chlorine. A pool was clearly inside. Khalifa walked the girls down the descending hallway and into the pool area where Pete and five black-cloaked persons with golden masks stood waiting for them.

Deep chills ran down Winter's back. The masks terrified the girls. In front of the cloaked figures, there stood some sort of altar of stone.

"Welcome," said a man's voice coming from a golden mask with a bloody handprint on it. "Welcome to the Plato Foundation. We rarely accept women, but you two are of use to us. We have studied you for years. This is your chance to make a difference. Are you in or are you dead? To be or not to be? That is not only Hamlet's query, it is The Epictetus Dilemma in your cases. Which do you choose?"

Julia didn't hesitate. "To be."

Winter, knowing she could not participate in this group, quietly stated, "I'm out." Her first thought was *I'd rather die.*

The leader in the mask with the bloody handprint instantly produced a pistol and shot to the right side of Winter, hitting a post behind her.

"I missed on purpose. I may or may not next time. Are you in or out?"

Winter had tears rolling down her eyes. She rethought. "I'm in."

"Ms. Thompson," said the leader . "To be or not to be?" This man sounded more dangerous than any person she had ever met.

"To be."

The fifth cloaked figure had a golden mask with a butterfly of gems covering his, her, or their face. A woman's voice sounded as she tilted her head to the right in a dark fashion, slow and terrifying, "I think you'll find our ways pleasant after tonight. You belong with us, Winter. Julia too. But, Winter, you are who we want most. Julia must know this from the start."

Winter sighed and cried harder. Her whole life, teachers favored her. It never won her friends. She loved to be loved and now law school was compromised perhaps. *Who were these people?*

"Who are you?" Winter asked out loud.

The lead cloaked figure shot to her right again. "No more questions. Now."

Pete moved swiftly across the cement and placed a black bag over Winter's head. She could not see what was happening to Julia. Winter's hands were zip-tied behind her, as were her legs together. Pete, she supposed it was, picked her up and dropped her in the pool.

I, Elle, can let you know the same thing was happening to Julia Saunders, but with Khalifa as the perpetrator. Pete was finishing his tasks with Winter.

Winter struggled. She could not think fast enough. Her legs would not separate. She could not use her hands. She could feel someone in the water now grabbing her. He was holding her down. Without thinking, she breathed in deeply and passed out as she drowned. The last words she had heard as she had been thrown in the pool was the fifth cloaked butterfly-masked figure who stated, "In the manner of Skull and Bones for these girls."

Chapter Eight
Awakening

Water sputtered from Winter as she coughed and spat onto the cement. She could see cloaked figures around her, and Pete was next to her. She hurt all over. There was shouting. Many people were in the pool arena, and she could see Professor Fouad. *Oh, thank you, God. Someone is stopping these people. Someone held me down. Maybe someone showed up and they had to save us.*

She felt a rush of adrenaline. She suddenly felt well. She tried to stand up, but Pete whispered, "You cannot yet stand up."

Incredulous, Winter said, "You tried to kill me."

"I did kill you. I'm your black mage, and I have now progressed, as have you."

Winter tried to stand up, but had to immediately lie back down. She sputtered again and water came from her inner region. Her lungs she supposed, but how it was possible to eject that much water was beyond her. She needed to tell the authorities here – the professors – what happened. She could see the dean.

"Winter," Pete commanded, "you are not among enemies. We have given you a great jump-start in life. I admit, I feel relieved. I didn't think you would be strong enough to live again, but the immortals always know best. I should have trusted the situation more. But it's over, and you are doing great. Julia, on the other hand, is dead, I'm sorry to tell you. I know you only knew her on a cursory basis, but this is always sad when it happens, and it only happens once every several decades or so. We weren't worried about Julia's will to live in this circumstance. We were worried about yours."

Winter tried to shout, "Murderers," to whomever would listen, but then she realized no police officer uniforms could be seen. No firemen attended the scene. The cloaked figures and six persons surrounded Julia's body. Khalifa was being given some sort of instructions.

"The immortals are usually still in ceremonial gear until you exit the building. Khalifa and I are your only direct contacts in these proceedings normally, but I know you can recognize the other figures present. You will not have a companion. Julia is gone."

Had she died and landed in hell? She could not understand why Pete was talking in such non-terrified tones about such madness. She scanned her life. She had done nothing wrong in her life. No alcohol for that matter. No drugs. No crime. No sin even. She was still a virgin at age twenty-eight. Mormonism was strict. She had been a notable educator in Utah where she was watched. A misstep would have been career suicide. She had not killed her career by crossing the church until after her last year teaching. She then disagreed with the church on a few issues, and she had been nearly excommunicated for being so vocal. But Mormons don't kill people for standing up for what they believe in – or for any reason for that matter.

Pete was crouched next to her. Soon, Dean Anderson was crouching next to Pete. "Winter, do you know who I am in regards to your life?"

Winter mustered strength. "Yes, Dean Anderson. Pete tried to murder me. They all murdered Julia, if she's dead."

"No one tried to murder you, Winter." Dean Anderson smiled kindly. In rather a chipper voice, Dean Cotton Anderson touched Winter's arm in a fatherly fashion. "These hazing parties are often ill-advised." Winter looked for another person for appeal and saw that the cloaked figures were gone. Only law school staff remained. "Tell her, Pete."

"This is the last time I will talk this directly about tonight," Pete said. "I will hopefully not ever explicitly address what happened here again. Things will not go well for you, I think, but you are in this for good. You will know the next step when it happens. We have infused your blood with whiskey. It's an ancient process. You'll be fine."

"Winter," Cotton Anderson said, and he had heard everything Pete said. "I think you are mistaken." Recognition of her situation started to dawn in Winter's mind. The law school had been aware of what happened tonight. They were going to cover it.

Winter looked: *The stone altar is gone*, she thought.

Soon, police and firemen and paramedics filled the pool area. A doctor was checking her. "This one is doing very well despite her alcohol content," the paramedic sort of chuckled in a knowing fashion and rambled about silly kids who tried to swim while drunk. He leaned down too close to her face, but in a congenial, lack-of-grace way said, "I'm so sorry about your friend."

Winter understood the danger of her situation. She was not going to be believed by authorities Pete attempted to murder her.

She woke up the next morning in a hospital bed. Yellow roses sat next to her bed from the law school, with a card which read, "Get well soon."

"You can go home today, honey." A nurse came into the room. "You are doing remarkably well for someone who drowned and was revived. I'm so sorry about the loss of your friend."

Had anyone contacted her emergency contact given to the school? Why hadn't her mom called? "Excuse me, have there been any calls – any visitors for me?"

"None, sweetheart. I'm so sorry. You really aren't that hurt. You just fell in the pool drunk. Your vitals are great. You can get dressed now. Your clothes from the night of your party are in that bag by the closet."

The nurse left. Winter felt remarkably good. She stood up and went to her plastic bag where she found the same sweatshirt, jeans, and Nikes she had worn to the pool, but they were new – an apparently unnoticed tag was still hidden in the back of the jeans. Winter dressed and started to leave. How would she get home? She didn't have a car whereas Pete had driven her to the "party." As she started to walk out of the hospital room, the nurse said, "Honey, you have forgotten your backpack and your roses."

"I'm sorry, ma'am, that's not my backpack."

"Oh, forgive me. A professor from St. Thomas brought it for you. I would take it." The nurse got serious. On her right wrist, she had an infinity tattoo that looked like an 808, and she pointed to it as if Winter would know what it meant. "Take it, dear," she said seriously.

Winter picked up the backpack and wrapped her right arm around the vase holding her yellow roses and started to leave.

"Sit in the wheelchair, sweetheart."

She was wheeled to the front door.

"Is someone picking me up?" Winter asked.

The nurse then whispered, "The keys to your new vehicle are in the front pocket of the backpack."

Chapter Nine:
New Universe

Winter pulled into the parking garage in the blue BMW coupe she had found parked where the card attached to the key said it was parked. Winter was confused, but she had actual knowledge that the men and women she now must count as associates were dangerous in ways she had never experienced in her life.

Was it the next morning? She checked the date. Saturday, nine October 2028. She had thought it was Monday and she needed to be at school. Only a few cars were in the garage of the law school. It was nine a.m. She parked. She grabbed the black backpack and sifted through it. A phone. A charger. A new laptop – a brand she had heard of but knew to be incredibly expensive: AEON. She found more cards. Why hadn't she gone through all of this immediately? She was still in shock, she realized. A black nondescript credit card with a business card paper-clipped to it in an envelope: limit US$65,000 and a note to go shop soon to update her wardrobe. "No one will ask questions." This was written underneath the command. Another business card: "Your apartment is fine. We like it, and we've already bugged it as needed. Please stay there unless you are at school or instructed to go elsewhere." Typed. Another card with passwords: "We've added satellite TV, a different TV, and some other equipment to your home" was written on the reverse. She had *died* for Netflix?

Winter wanted to go into the law school, find the dean, if

he was there on Saturday, and demand answers. The dean had heard Pete Johnson. They were part of this Plato Foundation. That girl, Julia, was dead. Should she go to the police?

Someone knocked on her window. Winter jumped and looked up to see Pete standing next to her BMW. She rolled down the window: "Pete, you are a murderer," Winter whispered the words. "How am I alive? I remember drowning. I remember dying."

Pete crouched near the driver's door. "Winter, that's not true. Look at me." Winter looked up against her will. "Say it, 'I did not drown. I was drunk and fell in the pool.'"

Winter decided to not fight. "I did not drown. I was drunk and fell in the pool."

"Good."

"I don't want this car."

"Winter, I can say this: you cannot fight. I am now what is called your mage. You have to obey me because when you fell drunk into the pool, I saved your life. You are scientifically beholden to me, and I own you: magic was done at the 'party' which bound you to me when I literally brought you back to life. I need to not talk about this," Pete gazed meaningfully at her. " I command you to keep the car, go shopping for clothes, and sleep today and tomorrow after shopping." Pete stood up and walked away.

Winter yelled, "Why wasn't Julia saved then?"

Pete just kept walking.

Winter picked up her phone and called the police – not 911. She googled the police department in Minneapolis and asked for a detective.

"Ah! Ms. Thompson! How are you feeling?"

"Sir, Julia Saunders was murdered."

Kind, jolly laughter met her. "Dear girl, the nurses have already informed us of what you've been saying. We have already investigated, and the case is closed. Julia tripped and fell into the pool while also having had too much to drink – now you stay off the sauce, young lady (the officer chuckled to himself again and Winter thought it was awful whereas Julia had died) – Khalifa Mohammed immediately jumped in to save Julia, and Peter Johnson immediately jumped in to save you. You were pulled out instantly, but Julia's t-shirt snagged on the air filter, and Mr. Mohammed had a difficult time getting her out. After Mr. Johnson got you out, he jumped in and helped Khalifa. Mr. Johnson then immediately presented you with CPR and Khalifa did the same for Julia. You were revived. Julia had already died and could not be revived. It was just the four of you there. You are not being charged for trespassing at the request of the dean of the law school, a friend of mine."

Julia knew better than to say that she had actually died underwater. What if she hadn't? What if she had just passed out?

"Sir, they zip-tied us and put bags over our heads. We were not drunk. There were five cloaked beings there."

More kind chuckling. "Ms. Thompson, the nurses also said you said this while sleeping. We have it on tape. No such thing happened."

Silence from Winter for a full minute. "Ms. Thompson?"

"This isn't true." Winter tried again.

"Dear, you've been through a lot. It's not a crime to be drunk near a pool, but you in particular should not drink. I'm sorry for the loss of your friend. I'm sorry, dear. I need to go."

"Thank you," Winter whispered and started to cry a bit. What had she done? She had agreed to be part of a frightening secret society. She then remembered the guns. She drove to the mall.

Chapter Ten
Dressing for Death

Winter went into Buckle and bought a new wardrobe. She didn't care what style The Plato Foundation wanted. These seemed like cute clothes to be regularly murdered in. Stylish yet comfortable. She stopped past Bloomingdale's and bought three dress suits, two pant suits, six shell shirts, two scarves, and four pairs of dress shoes for law school activities. She didn't even care what they looked like. She tried items for fit, and if it fit, she bought it. She stopped past REI and bought a huge North Face coat and some boots, three beanie hats with puffs, and gloves. The Mall of America was useful.

This took her five hours. She left and cried all the way home to Bloomington where she found her apartment altered as promised.

Chapter Eleven
Reaching 666

Hi, there. Elle Magellan. I'm cutting back to a view of the St. Thomas School of Law professors for a bit. Of note in this next part of my story is the fact that the men at St. Thomas didn't simply move on from Julia Saunders's death; they were experienced in death, and it did not affect them as it would have an average person. You'll see they did not mourn her loss in the same way others would have – as her family perhaps did. Perhaps not. Our ways are not the ways of most people.

James Madison jumped off the front step of his house in Minneapolis's older part of town and jauntily walked down the walkway of his yard to his 1967 Corvette Stingray. It did all right in the snow with the right tires, but the experience was worth taking an Uber in a big snowstorm. He loved October. Cool weather – the leaves changing. This was a great time of year anywhere in the northern part of the U.S.

The recruits had been gathered in various parts of the country. Rarely did they recruit anyone older than twenty-two. Few could handle it later, but the student Winter Thompson was of interest to Carlos Diaz, and one never questioned him. A former Mormon but of Jewish descent, Winter was brilliant, albeit her LSAT was only one hundred and fifty. Some felt she had found flaws in the examination and didn't know how to answer. Others said she didn't care, but this didn't fit her profile. Still some had thought maybe her IQ scores were too high perhaps. Still, no one – and I mean no one – ever argued with Carlos Diaz. The Foundation relied on his expertise to compete in world-level games of finance and war. No one knew money and death like the devil himself.

James Madison had been there the night the student Julia Saunders died. Madison had been cloaked but with no scripted lines. In such initiation circumstances, one only spoke if scripted. He also had been initiated in the drowning manner of Skull and Bones but had done so at the age of nineteen. He had been tapped in undergrad at an earlier age than some. Bright and wealthy, James Madison had seen much of the world through travel, and he felt confident in the systems to which his father, his grandfathers, and even one of his grandmothers had belonged. Women were rarely chosen. Madison pondered what was desired about Winter Thompson.

James Madison felt bad for Julia Saunders and her family who were wealthy and quite familiar with the techniques used in initiations into cohorts of the devil for business, politics, and more. But Winter's family was poor. Winter Thompson had had no indication prior to a month ago that such things existed. She had struggled not to tell her family. Winter Thompson was being watched closely by a team of six people who were known as watchers or caretakers – in addition to enjoying watching the kid, Pete Johnson, Winter Thompson was a strong personality James Madison enjoyed. He smiled to himself.

Everyone including James Madison had watched as Pete Johnson was beside himself trying to help Winter Thompson fight through her fears and still maintain decorum. Everyone could see Winter drove Pete mad sometimes. "Why can't we call the police again? They will listen to you." Pete was a mage and was able to command her not to call the police. Winter did not fully understand or believe if she did understand that she was forever beholden to her mage or wise old man figure who had literally killed her and brought her back to life using an ancient ritual known as Henge Seeking. The soon-to-be life-saving mage was technically called a person's Henge Mage, but Pete Johnson had perhaps wisely decided to not use the correct term right now with Winter, calling himself "her black mage or magician for answers."

"What answers?" was Winter's response most often.—

Again, the soon-to-be Henge Mage then runs the ceremony providing CPR and incantations needed in addition to the rituals provided by five higher Henge Mages. In a well-practiced method, , black mages (as opposed to white mages in other foundations) in the Plato Foundation help bring each other into the system.. There were many ways to kill and restart life. Drowning was chosen for Pete Saunders because he had been a lifeguard in Wyoming for many summers during his youth and college years in addition to being an aide for a Wyoming Supreme Court Justice. All preparations were thorough and intense. The ritual itself involved one sexual act between the bloody-handed masked leader and the fifth Henge Mage who Winter had not seen. Little did anyone know that the two were married (or that they were my husband and myself in Winter's case), but, despite this, outsiders would find the ritual offensive.

It was difficult to explain the ways of Henge and black magic and of centuries-old methods which had been passed down from generation to generation in Madison's family and the families of all his friends from Europe, Asia, Africa, and the Middle East. James Madison had never, though, seen an "outsider" brought in until watching Winter Thompson's experiences. Winter was struggling to understand and accept her fate. But Henge Mages actually "owned" their apprentice's will. The situation was safe. Madison had watched Pete have many meetings with Cotton Anderson who dictated many commands to give to Winter so she didn't destroy herself by looking crazy to everyone. Washington also guided Pete, whereas Washington was Pete's Henge Mage.

Madison wound through town while "Everybody Wants to Rule the World" by Tears for Fears played on the radio. He pulled into Oscar Fouad's house's driveway and honked lightly. Oscar ran out and got in the passenger side of the black car that smelled strongly of pine.

"I've been watching Winter and Pete this fine Saturday morning," Oscar laughed. "Pete can't get her to realize she is going to Las Vegas this weekend. He finally just commanded her. She just responded by saying he used the word 'command' a lot in a weird fashion."

"I saw some of it this morning. Not kidding. Those two are better than television." Madison shifted into reverse and backed out of the driveway. Today, the men were going to Thomas Magellan's home, the president of The Plato Foundation.

"I've only witnessed initiation not involving me once before. Last year. It's great to see again that while the Henge Mage has control, the true will of the person still shines through. Pete doesn't abuse his abilities, but honestly, Winter is a handful," Oscar said as he decided to use his seat belt, remembering as Madison drove that car safety was not Madison's favorite topic.

James Madison shifted his car into fourth, then fifth and drove out onto the interstate. They were headed to a neighborhood in Maple Grove where The Plato Foundation had a home for people who visited from out of town. Thomas Magellan was logistically located in New York, but he visited for new initiates. New magicians' initiations such as Winter's at the pool were staggered as to when they were admitted throughout the United States. October was a busy time for us, the Magellans because the games started in October, but most initiations happened in September. Winter's was late. Madison had questions. "I missed Pete and Winter's conversation last night. Did he explain future deaths?"

Oscar Fouad smiled and said, "He commanded her to listen to him. He sounds ridiculous when he says it. Not kidding: he makes me laugh. As I was watching, Pete actually looked directly where he knew a camera was last night after commanding her to listen and said openly to all of us watching, 'There has got to be a better way of saying this' and laughed. 'More deaths are coming,' Pete tried to explain to Winter."

Oscar continued, "Lucid and defiantly obedient, Winter yelled, 'Are you kidding with me?'

" 'No,' Pete then tried to carefully explain that her blood would be taken in Las Vegas and used to sort of 'kill' her – running her 'death number' up. She slapped him. She listened, but he had not commanded her to not slap him," Oscar laughed again.

"That one's sort of a surprise pistol," Madison commented.

"Sort of. She just wasn't raised knowing the dark magic ways. It must all be so shocking to her," Oscar Fouad mused.

Madison drove into The Plato Foundation's home. It had

a little plaque titled, "The Cottage House". Sane. Set. Stable. Madison loved his life and his associates.

Magellan opened the door into his warm, well-lit house as the night started to creep into the cool air and sky. "Welcome," he called openly to Madison and Fouad. "Take off your jackets. Leave your shoes at the door. Slippers are available if you so desire. Can I get either of you something to drink?"

"Whiskey." Madison took off his jacket revealing a Las Vegas T-shirt with his pair of jeans.

"Same." Oscar Fouad was also casually dressed. He also loved his life. Peaceful. Methodical. He knew what to expect and when.

Magellan indicated two whiskeys to a maid and walked with the men into the sitting room where five other men were seated around a piano and in varying chairs and couches. The room was quite large. I, Elle Magellan, walked in behind the two new guests and my husband, Thomas Magellan--whom I sometimes call "Magellan", and greeted Madison and Fouad as Magellan touched their shoulders to turn and talk with me, Elle. "I'll not be joining today. I understand Winter Thompson is the topic. She is adorable from what I hear." I rarely directly admit I watch everyone. The party all knew I saw everything – including in their lives. I exited.

"Yes," Madison laughed. "I am enjoying her on screen at least."

On the piano bench sat seventy-year-old English Alistair Tweed. Standing next to the fireplace mantel, a man named Oliver Material—sixty-two and bald, tall, and heavy--held a glass of wine. Richard Emerson sat in a chair to Material's left, next to the windows facing north. On the couch next to Emerson's chair also in front of the windows and to Emerson's left were Cotton Anderson and Franklin Washington. Madison and Fouad each took chairs to the right of Alistair Tweed or Salty, as he was called. Magellan pulled in two chairs from the dining room, bringing one for Material if he desired and one for himself by the entrance to the sitting room. Cotton Anderson stood up and shook Magellan's hand. "I didn't get a chance to greet you, Thomas. I haven't seen you in ages. Elle looks happy and well."

"She does, doesn't she?" Magellan gladly and familiarly shook hands with Anderson.

"Well," Thomas Magellan stated. "I am positive Winter will not be able to identify me as the lead Henge Mage in her initiation ceremony for some time. I will not introduce myself to her as such until she has passed five hundred and fifty-five deaths, which could take three years or so as you know. She is doing great."

The men all chuckled softly. "And congratulations to Madison and Fouad who have both passed six hundred and sixty-six deaths. As we all know, the last set of deaths until six hundred and sixty-six can take various amounts of time depending on the players and the circumstances.. We are here to celebrate that tonight. Immortal, are we?"

"Some say so," Madison whispered the expected response.

"Some say so," Fouad also said.

"*Some say so* is correct. You are both known to Carlos Diaz, and you should know great things are expected of you both. This small pocket of Plato mages at St. Thomas School of Law is beloved by all in our Foundation."

Thomas Magellan raised his glass. "To immortality and making a difference."

"To immortality and making a difference," the men all replied.

"It is important that Winter is not ever introduced to Elle while in Las Vegas: she must never even see her. Elle is her historian. Watching is difficult to deal with. Also, try not to let her know you see her and Pete's story."

None of the men laughed. "As you all know, the final round means death to any player who is not clear. Every other year or so, someone dies in the lower rounds. All the way dead. Died squared.

Tomorrow we leave for Las Vegas for the beginning of The Epictetus Dilemma. Remember that to play without a clear conscience with Carlos Diaz is to play to lose and cause harm to everyone. Make sure you are all clear before heading to Las Vegas tomorrow. The trip is also a celebration for Madison and Fouad, and we will have their assignments soon."

Cotton Anderson leaned forward. "We'd like to keep them here if possible."

"Totally possible. We understand the close-knit cohort we have going here and don't wish to rock the boat." Magellan smiled.

The doorbell rang. Magellan laughed, "This must be Pete and Khalifa."

Elle Magellan answered the door. The men in the sitting room could hear laughter and joyous greetings before Pete and Khalifa sheepishly walked into the room. The eight men there laughed. "Go get two chairs from the dining room," commanded Franklin Washington, Pete's Henge Mage. Both boys went. Khalifa's Henge Mage was Alistair Tweed, formerly from Notre Dame.

Henge Mages did not always follow their apprentices past

three hundred and thirty-three deaths, but both Khalifa and Salty ended up at St. Thomas, and both were happy. "Go get a chair," Salty called after Khalifa just for good measure.

"Well," Magellan said in the silence after the younger men sat down. "How is it going?"

All of the men quietly chuckled. "I sound ridiculous every day," Pete moaned. The men laughed.

"It will get better. Ease up on her. You've commanded so very much, you will end up having to un-command – to make a word – yourself so Winter will be capable of any independent thought," Washington told Pete

James Madison's mage was Cotton Anderson, a very high-ranking man in The Plato Foundation, and Oscar Fouad's was Richard Emerson. Oliver Material was the banker for the group, and he did not participate in mage–apprentice creations, but his mage was rumored to be Magellan. This was, if so, considered a fully stacked room where every Henge Mage was with one of their apprentices – a powerful scenario for finding truth using seer stones.

Death was familiar to these men. Still, Salty Tweed commented, "We should remember the life of Julia Saunders."

"Hear, hear," said the various men. No one chuckled. No one took death lightly in this room. They were quite familiar with death, but so much so that it did not phase them in the same way it did others.

"To Julia Saunders."

"To Julia Saunders."

"To Pete and Khalifa."

"To Pete and Khalifa."

Apprentices worked in pairs until they passed six hundred and sixty-six deaths. Immortals worked alone. James Madison turned to Oscar Fouad, his longtime partner, and they touched glasses. "To infinity," James Madison said.

"To infinity," Oscar replied.

At this point, Magellan produced a small seer stone. "Let's ask Carlos Diaz what true will exists for James Madison and Oscar Fouad."

The stone was a brown, flat, oval marble stone. Thomas Magellan laid it on the table and said an incantation: "*Bashaq dah bashaq doh.*" This meant, *In addition, two more.* "*Besha di, bashaq doh? Sandaz doh via. (What are their true wills? We have sacrificed two lives to know this.) The lives were attempted to be reclaimed and added to the great conversation, but we lost one.*" The last part of the incantation was spoken in English.

A star made from light arose from the stone. This sign meant Carlos Diaz was also reading his stone wherever he was in the world at the time; he would have known the time of the scheduled incantation. Oscar Fouad's name rose like smoke. The words *U.S. Constitution Law Professor* rose. Then *Notre Dame*. This was his final true will or calling in his life. James Madison's name arose, then *U.S. Supreme Court Justice*. These were final estimations of abilities, and the Foundation was committed to making it happen. And had the means. *Welcome, Winter Thompson's Henge Mage Mr. Johnson. Welcome, Wounded Henge Mage, Mr. Mohammed.* Julia Saunders's name rose: *R.I.P.*

The stone shuddered on the table and all light and smoke dispersed. "So be it," said Thomas Magellan.

"So be it," said all in the company.

Silence filled the room. The title of Wounded Henge Mage was a blessing to Khalifa. It meant he had reached the stage of

Henge Mage and did not have to do the stage again. Carlos Diaz was also sending Khalifa on a different path which meant he would have to return home to Abu Dhabi after law school to regroup. But that's another story. Wounded Henge Mages became health doctors. Always.

I, Elle, stepped into the quiet room. "Dinner is set."

"Ah," Richard Emerson said: "Delightful as always."

Chapter Twelve
Las Vegas

Peter and Winter walked into the front entrance of the Bellagio and worked their way to the foyer whose ceiling was designed by Chihuly. Winter was whispering in an angry voice, "I don't understand what you mean by 'more deaths'." A look of real terror crossed her eyes.

"It will just be like bad dreams; I promise."

"What does that mean? I have already dreamt so much about, I don't know, drowning in a pool a month ago. I'm serious. I'm terrified."

"I would be lying to say nothing physical will happen to you going forward, but the early deaths are psychological fitness in their trials and not physical. We use ancient voodoo practices. Your blood is "killed." We use incantations to assign your blood to an object such as a small figurine or statue. We then, in your name, destroy the figurine, "killing" it and your blood attached to it in a vial. When your blood is "killed," you actually die for a split second, and you, in turn *dream* about the death, You will see in your mind your deaths." Pete was intensely whispering. He knew others would be watching their interaction even though they may not be able to hear quite well through their phones in such a busy place. Fame of his inability to control his apprentice had been moved throughout the foundations under Carlos Diaz. This meant Plato from Rome,

Skull and Bones from Yale, Westfield from Harvard, Carnegie from MIT, Allice from UC Fullerton (few knew this organization swayed many policies in the United States), Osiris from Princeton, Horus from Columbia, and possibly more knew he was in over his head with a relentlessly aggressive questioner as an apprentice, and Pete was beside himself. Pete had crossed five hundred and fifty-five deaths and was going to start the ten-year process of reaching six hundred and sixty-six tonight. His entrance exam to enter this stage? Kill and revive.

All business. Pete Johnson had been taught by his incredibly wealthy father that magic was always all business and feeling differently was a notable mistake. His father loved his mother, but even their relationship was all business. Pete could tell their love for each other was a mutual respect for the other's love of the games in life. Pete, on the other hand, found himself in wonder almost every day at the glowworm in his care. Hadn't Winston Churchill called himself a glowworm in a world of worms? Winter Thompson was a glowworm he could not control. *Thank God for magic*, Pete thought. He had it, and he had to use it.

"I want a separate room," Winter protested.

"No," Pete tried to sound final. As they reached the checkout counter, Pete was terse with the somewhat jolly desk attendant who was arranged as one of the coordinators of the foundation conference for the biggest groups of power ever existing in the United States. The attendant seemed to understand Pete's problem *before* they reached the counter. *Who knows I can't control her without demanding it?* Pete wondered. Apparently "George", his name tag said, did.

"Hey, there," George said rather cheerily.

"I want my own room," Winter leaned up on the counter.

"She wants her own room," George helped. He smiled from ear to ear at Pete.

"No. We're together."

"We're not."

Pete could not command her to obey in public. Pete had forgotten to command her to sleep in the same room with him before they reached the hotel. He could not keep up with the amount of commands he needed to give her.

He had commanded her not to ever say, "Aren't you going to command me?" or anything of the sort.

Just then, Cotton Anderson appeared. He was also all smiles and tried to explain to Winter that the Foundation needed to save money – clearly not true. "You need to stay with Pete." Winter did not want to cross the dean of the law school, so she backed down. Pete stood with his head down.

"One room!" George was flourishing his hands as he typed Pete's name into the computer. "Ah. Here we are. Pete Johnson's name. You and Winter Thompson are in room 504."

All foundation people knew floors two through eight meant higher power. Guests wanting to feel special stayed high in Las Vegas. All of the dangerous action happened on the second to eighth floors.

The entire casino was filled with young and higher players, as world death gamers were called. The Plato Foundation had six hundred and sixty-six members, as did all of the foundations – an important number. The casino was full. Seven foundations made up the Diaz–United States Star Cohort. No one knew how many cohorts Satan ran, but the Star Cohort was the highest in the United States. The four thousand six hundred and sixty-two guests were housed throughout

Vegas on and off throughout the week depending on the need to be there. The Plato Foundation was housed at the Bellagio where they were hosting various meetings and events including the year's end final poker game. Death poker involved shuffled (loaded) pistols and talking. No one had died squared in over thirty years at the year-end games. Clear players live. Cloudy players die. Apprentices never played at this level but were there to learn. Plato had seven new apprentices from various Catholic universities across the United States. Members in general ranged in age from twenty to eighty-nine. The Immortal Games' apprentices came to Vegas jokingly telling their schoolmates they were going to run the Boston Marathon or train for it. They weren't. All trip goers were fit enough to run it, though. Winter included, albeit barely.

Peter Johnson and Winter Thompson walked together, with Peter carrying his and Winter's carry-ons, toward the elevator when they ran into Khalifa Mohammed. "Khalifa, where are you housed?"

"Next door."

"Let me have your room, and you can room with Pete." Winter tried to get Khalifa to understand her plea.

Khalifa laughed, "No, Miss Winter. How will I bring a girl back to my room?" Everyone knew Khalifa was forbidden to have premarital sex, but he joked about it with many Americans.

"Winter," Pete now could talk to Winter. "I command you to stay with me in my room and not complain."

Khalifa smiled and winked at Pete. "Have fun. Don't do anything I wouldn't do."

"Guaranteed," Pete responded.

"I'm this way right now," Khalifa headed off.

Pete uncharacteristically took Winter's hand, and they headed into the elevator. An attendant took them to the fifth floor. As they entered their room, Winter sat on her bed and started to cry.

"I cannot have sex. I cannot break all Mormon laws even if I have left."

"We aren't having sex."

"Good."

"Good. It's settled. But we're sleeping in this bed together. I am not sleeping on a cot."

"Fine."

"Good."

Winter opened the closet to find a wardrobe with her name on the tags. Pete had the same. A Versace gown she could have never afforded was accompanied by Jimmy Choo shoes.

"That's for Tuesday night. Don't wear it until then. Leave it in there." *Can a command be implied?* Pete wondered. "I command," he added.

James Madison smoked a cigarette while watching Pete and Winter on his laptop from his Bellagio room. "When are we going to let him know?"

Cotton Anderson, standing next to Madison, said, "Tonight. We'll tell him tonight he can command her also by just using her nickname which we established."

"What is the nickname?"

"Ace."

Madison laughed. "He has to call her Ace?"

"That's the plan."

"Send him a text explaining. Let's let him know now, Anderson." Madison fought for Pete.

57

Winter walked into the bathroom and Pete looked at his phone and then looked at the television and flipped it off with his left hand. Cotton Anderson and James Madison laughed.

Winter begged to try on the Versace gown, and Pete gave into her pleadings and now commanded her to try on the dress. Winter came out of the bathroom wearing her pretty black three-quarters dress. "Ace, you look beautiful, but you have to put that back until Tuesday," Pete then said.

Winter started to unzip it from behind but couldn't as she walked back to the bathroom. "Could you fix this?" she asked Pete. Anderson and Madison laughed harder.

"Yes," Pete whispered, and he moved over to Winter, and unzipped the gown. Winter went into the bathroom.

Winter came out in a skirt, NY T-shirt, and a pair of Converse boat shoes. Las Vegas was cooler, but not cold. She grabbed a Gucci casual jacket, and said to Pete, "I'm headed down to the casino."

"Hell, no, Ace."

Richard Emerson had now joined Madison and Anderson watching the two. They all laughed.

"Ace?" Winter furrowed her eyebrows.

"Not by yourself, you're not. The casino floor games are games of numbers: poker, Black Jack, roulette. We do not play the numbers this trip; we play the deaths to live. Correction: I play the deaths. You play nothing until you pass five hundred and fifty-five safety deaths."

"I don't understand how I can pass five hundred and fifty-five deaths. How many times have I died beyond falling in the pool?"

"Remember, Ace, we say that you have never died falling in the pool. You fell in the pool drunk and were saved. We'll know more when we take your blood in about twenty minutes. Just hang tight here in the room, Ace. We have to do a few things. Deaths mean life. Repeat after me, Ace: Death means life."

"Death means life."

"Our ways are life-saving." Pete waited. Winter said nothing. "Say it, Ace."

"Our ways are life-saving."

"Winter, it will be okay," Pete said softly. He was worried that her feisty anger had turned a bit to soft fear.

Emerson, Anderson, and Madison dressed and left Madison's room.

Twenty minutes or so later, a knock on the door was heard, and was opened to a phlebotomist.

"Sit down, Ace."

"I don't like being called Ace."

"You love me calling you Ace, Ace."

The phlebotomist was clearly laughing at Pete's handling of Winter. Most apprentices were familiar with protocols and didn't fight every request turned into a command to deal with the constant contrary ideals. Winter sat obediently and listened to instructions. It shocked both Pete and the phlegotomist. One bag of blood would do it. The knock on the door came again, and Pete opened to room service: caprese and coffee. Everyone was in a great mood. *Super*, thought Pete. Food always came with a blood draw in Plato.

The phlebotomist did a few calculations with blood samples, a microscope, and his laptop.

"She'll be good to pass two hundred and twenty-two by the time she leaves Las Vegas."

"No." Pete looked concerned. "She won't understand."

59

Chapter Thirteen
The Game at Play: The Epictetus Dilemma

Franklin Washington and Oscar Fouad joined James Madison, Richard Emerson, and Cotton Anderson. "The problem we are seeing with Winter is that she wasn't raised in our ways. But she is under contract," Washington said to the men as they sat down to dinner in the casino's Le Cirque restaurant. There were private restaurants on higher floors, but the men always frequented Le Cirque once a year. The chef was friends with Emerson. The chef had stopped his process at five hundred and fifty-five.

"She's under contract?" Emerson queried.

"She's under contract." Cotton Anderson confirmed.

"Thank God. I thought maybe Thomas was getting too bold for all of us. Who are her parents?"

"She's six generations away from *any* participation. They just haven't been called in for over one hundred years. The information seems to have been lost in her family. She talks to her parents once every other day, and they wanted to know why she drank at the party, etc. – stick to Mormon ways is their suggestion – and they seem wholly unaware of the true will ways," Washington continued. "Also, they do not know they are Jewish."

"The last name," Madison commented.

"Yes, but there are Jewish without Jewish names. We have a genealogical chart for Winter Thompson tracing back six hundred years following through two Jewish lines both of which lead back to pure Roman lines who made deals with the devil." Washington told the waiter his order.

"She's generational which makes her under contract with Carlos Diaz from birth," Cotton Anderson explained. "Carlos Diaz commanded us to bring her in: she's an only child. I just got a text that she's strong enough to make it to two hundred and twenty-two by Tuesday night. Her nightmares should not be any different than another apprentice, but new apprentices – who you all know are rare – have terrible nightmares. Whereas there has been a gap in service from her ancestors, her nightmares might have to compensate for the lack of payment for generations. They might be terrible."

"As you all know, science dictates payments to Carlos. Somewhere, all of our ancestors made deals with the devil, selling all future generations in a contract to Satan. It's our way," Cotton Anderson continued. It's considered kind in Plato to re-explain to younger kings or players what may have been forgotten.

"It's our way," Emerson resounded. Although none of them would admit it, their ways were painful to the men. But they were bound. Winter was bound. All of them were generationally "cursed" to serve mankind in these death-inducing ways. As was the case with all participants, they found pride in their courage.

Carlos Diaz was confusing to some mages. Many found Diaz flat-out delightful, but Washington and Anderson knew in particular how fiercely unkind Satan could be. Carlos Diaz was incredibly civil, well-mannered, seemingly kind, beautiful, stunning, startling, and dangerous when running events. But if crossed, Carlos Diaz could be bloody and mean. Still, they were bound to be a participant. Their fathers had given them up to play later. If the general public knew of this world, everyone in the United States would want to be the players in the death games in Vegas this weekend, but everyone in Vegas knew the personal emotional payments needed if "under contract" were higher than average men and women would know. A lot higher. Their lives were exciting. But their lives were dangerous and sometimes terribly sad. The men at Le Cirque knew how tragic Julia's death was, but if they continually mourned sadness, they would be paralyzed and of no use to Carlos. No one wanted that. The men and one woman in the St. Thomas School of Law members of the U.S. Roman Catholic Plato cohort (Thomas and I came from St. Thomas) had learned to find joy in each other's company and loyalty. A few other cohorts – Westfield, Skull and Bones, and Osiris – were also represented at St. Thomas School of Law in the faculty and student body, but The Plato Foundation held the reins of leadership at the law school and the larger university. Winter Thompson was now number six hundred and sixty-five – not in deaths – in placement in The Plato Foundation. Winter Thompson would have been six hundred and sixty-six if Julia Saunders had lived, but an empty seat was awarded to Carlos Diaz to fill as he desired. The men had no idea if someone from St. Thomas School of Law would be picked to replace Julia Saunders.

Carlos Diaz had no such plans. While at dinner, Anderson received word that six hundred and sixty-six was an African-American girl at Notre Dame who had bloodlines unparalleled and was well versed in the ways of true will. She willingly died and was easily restored. No drama. Others were equally talking about how a no-drama girl was perhaps more needed than Winter Thompson.

Blood. Blood mattered. Not race. Not looks. Blood and past dangerous covenants. Some blood could withstand the deaths more than others. Blood designations in these matters were very secret: male blood was found to withstand the deaths more than female. Winter Thompson's blood was very strong, the men would have all known. . When a Henge Mage and an apprentice relationship was formed through black magic, the deaths, as they were called, made very powerful people not only who could survive death, but who gained charm, persuasive abilities, and stunning beauty. Some claimed these were gifts for obedience from Carlos. Magellan, in so deep genealogically – is what "in so deep" meant to these men and me, Elle – that he personally conversed with the devil himself on a weekly basis, made it clear to his acquaintances and friends that it was all scientific. Incantations and more were just undiscovered science, he reminded all of the men (and me) under his tutelage.

The men sipped wine. "The games start in two hours."

Here's the gig: Deaths are a commodity in Carlos Diaz's world. The more one dies or kills, the more power, gravitas, wealth, beauty, and dangerous qualities Carlos Diaz bestows on the victim or the killer, especially after a participant dies or kills (worth five deaths) six hundred and sixty-six times.

Each cohort's members sought to die six hundred and sixty-six times through voodoo-like methods where blood was attached to a figurine of the subject at hand through a vial, an incantation was said, and then the figurine was destroyed (and through other means after five-hundred and fifty-five). It was documented for thousands of years that a nightmare haunts the owner of the blood symbolically and literally deceased. The nightmare or "daymare" as is often the case is simply an image in one's mind of the death happening from one's own eyes. A person whose blood figurine is being beheaded will "dream" of being beheaded. Physically, if one has been initiated into a magician's life, death passes in an instant and mild discomfort is felt.

Seer stones confirm the number of deaths a person has survived.. Blood type TGVX has been found to be most associated with the strongest "dreamers".

An *apprentice dreamer* dies through voodoo deaths until two hundred and twenty-two. *Seasoned dreamers* also die through voodoo deaths but through deaths which must be coordinated one at a time per day unlike the apprentice deaths which can be done many each day one after the other until five hundred and fifty-five, at which point a seasoned dreamer becomes a *player* and must be shot or hung or otherwise physically killed in reality to increase his or her death number. Those who die and live until six hundred and sixty-six deaths are *unseated kings* or *unseated king starlets* (those who identify as female) who must then go through a hero's journey to become *a seated king* or *king starlet*. Kings and king starlets are invincible.

Winter was scheduled to have two hundred and twenty-two figurines destroyed "in her name" before Tuesday. It was Sunday, James Madison and Oscar Fouad were being made unseated kings in hell on Tuesday.

Dreamers could handle more numbers of deaths closer to their initial murder than later. During this honeymoon period, nightmares did not seem to bother TGVX-blooded persons much beyond a horror film's results. Mind you, forty-eight hours of horror films, but still doable. At two hundred and twenty-two, a new "hat" was given to each apprentice-turned-dreamer. It took two additional years to reach five hundred and fifty-five, and a variety of times to reach six hundred and sixty-six, then years to establish well oneself as a noted king. Being "clear" – or honest was the best way to put it – secured not dying. Honesty and loyalty were the two highest desired qualities in the star network.

There was a lower caste, also. The 808 caste was created by Carlos Diaz to serve the kings, as some referred to the cohorts.

In 808, girls were made queens, and queens were for dangerous chess. Queens stopped at death five hundred and fifty-five. Queens did not attend the games in Las Vegas. Some girls became kings by becoming players and passing five hundred and fifty-five: girl kings were called *king starlets*. It was still unforeseen what Winter would be, but she was currently believed to possibly be a future king starlet whereas Carlos had invited her to Las Vegas. It was rumored Queen Elizabeth II of the United Kingdom had been a King Starlet player until her Platinum Jubilee at which time she retired from gaming.

Death poker consisted of men and women, each with a pistol with a silencer, gathering in a room on the fifth floor. Seven players were allowed in each round; all sat in chairs in a circle with a table next to them to rest their pistol if they desired. Deaths from five hundred and fifty-five to six hundred and sixty-six were physical deaths trusting that the system worked. It always did, unless it didn't. Men died if not "clear" – but because of their magical initiations, they felt the death only for an instant. Men shot each other to obtain their higher numbers. Their powers could not be touched by white magicians who refused to die. (White magicians are very powerful in their way. But that is an entirely different story.)

In a death poker game, a dealer "dealt" a sentence. For instance, the "deal" could be, "The US Supreme Court should have twelve justices instead of nine." That would be the deal. The players then staked up to five lives (shots) and dealt themselves into the great conversation. Sides on all deals were established almost immediately but were often predicted in advance by the powers that be. Players that made a grammatical mistake or used a logical fallacy died. Died –but so quickly and revived so quickly as to not be noticed by the untrained eye. The rules were so infinite so as to make it impossible to explain here, but for example, if two opposing players argued against each other, and one player used a straw man argument, his or her opponent could call him or her on it and shoot them. Dead. Most players could handle five deaths a deal. Good players got their deaths elsewhere (skiing, skydiving, ocean swimming, rock climbing, and more – good players tried not to die and if they fell behind their target naturally, they knew what to do). Players died for seconds at a time. But they flatlined. No blood. It was proven. Persons between five hundred and fifty-five and six hundred and sixty-six deaths were on their way to immortality – if clear enough.

How did they dare play in Vegas in October? They had already killed once and resurrected once to become a Henge Mage, another name for player. Before the first deal, shots were fired on the roof. Ten new Plato Henge mages were taken to the roof and *shot*. All had lived in the last thousand years for Plato. Plato seemingly never had a "bad tap" as it was called when a person seemingly survived the nightmares and helped to resurrect a person after killing them themselves but did not survive the first shot..

Carlos Diaz seemingly liked death. But, Magellan argued, it was the necessary way to make a difference when there was no other way. For these men bound by generations past, there was no other way.

The first deal tonight was unknown to players, but Washington was a dealer, and he knew it to be "Epictetus the slave belonged to a natural aristocracy". Gamers would gather in the Bellagio tonight.

"The first shot is in twenty minutes. We need to hurry up there. Washington and Tweed, do you have your pistols on you? Pete and Khalifa will be up there. Khalifa won't play past the first shot in the games albeit he will do sport to run his number up." Anderson talked with familiarity.

All of the men stood up at once. Some placed their napkins next to their plates. Some sipped wine. Madison had whiskey.

In a world run by Carlos Diaz, the only question or dilemma was to be or not to be. Shakespeare was very familiar with the game. The same game was given different names each year and ended on Christmas Eve. The games began midnight on October 13 and lasted throughout the fall until the winter equinox, always celebrated Christmas Eve midnight. This year's game was called The Epictetus Dilemma in honor of the slave Greek teacher, Epictetus. In a way, all of these men and women were enslaved to Carlos Diaz. In one way or another.

The shots were off. No ceremony precluded the shots so as to not make the often, somewhat terrified, mostly 23-year-olds nervous. Winter would be over thirty when facing her first shot. Pete was five years younger than she was. Five shot men and five shot women (an even number this year) stood unharmed. Quiet applause and laughter came from the newly minted players.

What's the answer to the Epictetus Dilemma of whether or not to live? That answer was always, "To be. To live well."

Magellan asked the new players if they wanted to be or not be. "To be. To live well," they were required to say and did. Carlos Diaz ran organizations of pomp and circumstance. Lines mattered.

Chapter Fourteen
Poker Game

Immortals could take infinite shots at a time. It was rare when this happened. Players could only take five to fifteen shots a night depending on strength of blood. Lights above the seats indicated the judges' judgment: green meant right to shoot and red meant fair game to be hit by the person with a green light. Players had watches that indicated the same, but players who were above five hundred and ninety were well-versed in death opportunities and voids as missed shots or correct answers were called in the case of correct answers.

The St. Thomas School of Law Plato men attended Pete's first round. Pete was dressed in formal casual – in a very nice suit without a tie. Winter was back in their room watching *That Touch of Mink*. At seven a.m., her nightmares would begin. There's no way to explain this to people prior to experiencing it or watching it themselves. It's as if the person is being tortured but no one can be seen torturing the apprentice. Khalifa came with them. Khalifa would now go home – it was decided – instead of finishing law school, regroup with his family, and then, if they so desired, he would return to go to medical school at Harvard.

Elsewhere, Pete's attendant was preparing to send a hundred very small figurines of Venus named Winter Thompson with her blood attached around the small statue into a cement mixer. It sounds archaic, but it works if the apprentice has been initiated into the star network.

This is Elle. I journaled as Winter "dreamt" for the first time as we supposed. Here were my notes:

Like with voodoo, what is done to the doll happens to the apprentice. Death by crushing suffocation will be her dreams over and over tonight until she wakes in a sweat usually. She technically will have died one hundred times by the moment she wakes through her alarm at five p.m. It takes about ten hours to dream out a hundred early deaths for the average player. As the deaths increase in number, strength increases, but so does the need to actually physically die to obtain an opportunity for death.

I'm Elle still. I'm just going to comment here about Winter's appearance. As I see it, women are comparable to animals' physiques. Some women have the physique equivalent to the strength of a little bird. Some have the strength of a lion. I have been compared to a tiger. I am not a small woman, but I am incredibly fit and considered stunningly beautiful. Winter is comparable to a thoroughbred horse. She is sleek looking and strong.

I speak in past tense unless needed otherwise. Back to the story.

Pete sat with six other newly-minted players. They had changed. Head shots or chest shots were the only shots allowed. To shoot otherwise was to obtain a red light. Suits were expensive in this world, and bullet holes were real. Shirts could be switched out with less cost, albeit still expensive.

The dealer sat in the circle of eight and said, "Epictetus belonged to a natural aristocracy."

Pete "dealt" in first. "Agreed." Also, the five judges for

each round voted immediately and used seer stone indicators to see if each player told the truth as perceived by the player – truth was sometimes subjective (but not always). A green light showed independent of a red light. Only a red light accompanied by a green light allowed a player to shoot. Red–green meant "a shot will be fired: the green light will shoot the red light." Green alone meant "the speaking player is clear/is telling the truth to Carlos Diaz." Red alone never exists. Once a red light appears, simultaneously a green light appears indicating shooting. Failure to shoot during a red-green scenario results in the lights flipping: shooters have five seconds. Failure to shoot in a flip results in a fold from both, now disqualified, flipped players. All previous numbers are suspended during a game. A shot is a shot. In life, a higher numbered player is not able to be killed by a lower numbered player. Pride is also on the line in such games.

Oh. Killing gives the shooter five deaths himself – but he feels it. Physical strength matters . It pays to be good – to be mentally and physically fit.

Three players agreed. Green lights all. Three remaining players disagreed, two green clears and one red light. Pete had five seconds to shoot the dishonest player who was betraying Pete's side by telling a lie. Pete shot him. The "wounded" kid looked down. He was alive. His opportunity for death as it is called had worked. The new players all knew the first shot had been survived, but they had had to go through massive efforts to resurrect an apprentice just recently and it was still strange to realize that they had reached in infantile form of immortality through years of dying in dreams.

Pete played again. "Thoreau indicates with the woodcutter that some persons are naturally grand, king-like, intelligent beyond circumstances." Green. "*Walden*."

A player from China from Horus named Xi said, "Yes, but poor circumstances indicate a lack of aristocratic tendencies needed for success. Poverty itself plays as an indication of lack of nobility." Green showed throughout his argument.

"Not so," said Pete. Green. "Jungian and Campbell archetypes portray the fact that an impoverished person can cross the abyss to wealth if he or she has the will." Green throughout.

It didn't matter what was said. It only mattered that the speaker truly believed what he or she was saying and that it was correctly said. Honesty, lack of logical fallacies, clarity and grammar were the real games of life and death in the star networks. Lying to one's self was lying to Carlos Diaz, and lying meant death. As the network saw it, this method created conversations which were the purest in finding the best answer.

Failure to deal beyond agreement or disagreement meant folding. Common in these first rounds, a few brave souls spoke while the others became emotionally accustomed to the idea of being or not being. To be was always the best answer.

In the end, Pete and Xi were in a stalemate. Three other players failed to deal in, except for the kid who had been shot who was forced to defend Pete or be shot again. He did defend Pete, but he faced a logical error using a correlation as a causation example, and Xi shot him. He dealt in again, and gained a reputation for humility, but lied again, this time the truth disagreeing with Pete, and Pete had to shoot him. In the end, Steve, as his name was, folded. The room applauded him with quiet chuckles.

Pete and Xi had a one-hour conversation with continual green lights and no shots. The game was called a tie, and both men were applauded.

This is death poker. It continues outside of Las Vegas. The Great Conversation as it is called is experienced in alleyways and in law schools at night and during the day. A red-green situation results in someone getting shot at one point or another. The difference is that once the game is literally "afoot" as opposed to in the casino, shooters had twenty-four hours to kill. Players still only die for a second and then revive. Sometimes, though, non-players died square. In such a case, the ability to contain the situation matters a great deal. To expose the game in any way is to lose on behalf of your cohort. Exposure means loss. A great deal of money and political posts were on the line.

Two rounds were played before a final round. Logic scores also indicated final players. Neither Pete nor Xi felt a shot beyond the first shot on the roof under a tent to protect anonymity and prying newspaper eyes from wondering why men were shooting youth on a roof. Both had perfect logic scores, perfect grammar, and perfect clarity until the final round. Xi became sloppy in fatigue and Pete shot him winning the five hundred and fifty-five rounds. Elsewhere in the building, 590s, 600s, 620s, also played. Immortals played the same deal on Monday night. The night ended at six a.m.

"You better run up there, champ," said Washington to Pete. "She starts to dream in less than an hour."

Pete shook hands with Magellan, who then told Pete to sprint. When Pete reached the hotel door, he knocked first and came in to find Winter asleep on the bed. He admitted to himself, the seer stone tells me, he liked her. He was attracted to her. "Winter," he said rather loudly. *Hopefully*, Pete thought, *if I quit babying her, we would cease to be the whole of the seven-star network's reality show.*

Winter sat up. "Hey. Where have you been Being awake

for the dreams was not a problem. The dreaming was terrible, though. "Winter, you need to come with me."

Washington had prepared a room for Winter's dreaming. It was in a house off of Flamingo about four miles from I-15 heading right.. It usually took over an hour for the worst to happen, so, it was best to wait to take dreamers to padded rooms until the last minute.

Soon, Washington, Madison, and Magellan were at the door. "Ace, you need to come with us." Winter crawled out of bed still fully clothed, put on her boat shoes, and went with Pete and the men.

Chapter Fifteen
The Path to Becoming a Dreamer

When the hallucinations began, Winter surprised everyone by simply sitting on the floor of the padded room and then actually sleeping on the floor.

The men stood in front of the screen watching her room and Washington said, "Someone check to see if her statues are in the cement."

Magellan turned to Pete. "I thought you said she was terrified about the concept of voodoo deaths."

"I called them 'more deaths'. She was terrified. I see my mistake. I tried to tell her it would only be like having bad dreams."

"That isn't quite correct either," Madison laughed.

"They're in!" someone yelled back through a switchboard. "What the hell is going on? Have I got someone else's blood?" The voice through the switchboard was now yelling at someone near him in another location, then back to Magellan. "I'm not kidding! Is there some not-so-innocent player getting free deaths?"

"It's Winter Thompson's. We promise," Magellan assured them. "I brought it to you myself. Something is going on here. No one sleeps the first round of dreams."

"That girl is not average," Pete commented quietly.

The men smiled to themselves.

The game would not be afoot until after the immortals played tomorrow night. No shots were ever shot among the immortals. They were too good. The Great Conversations or final poker games, though, were powerful and worth witnessing. They moved quickly, and green continually shone above all chairs. As a result, the final round was often called The Green Hand or The Green Lights.

Thomas Magellan laid his seer stone on the switchboard counter. "Holy Guardian Angel," Magellan requested. An angel symbol floated from the stone in light. "Winter Thompson's death number this morning." The number sixteen rose, then seventeen, eighteen. A pause happened. Then nineteen.

This is Elle. It's important to note that my husband asked the stone's angel to state Winter's death number just that night.

"Holy shit," said Oscar Fouad. "She's dreaming incredibly fast. At this rate, she'll hit hundred far before five p.m."

"Is she passed out, do you think?" Washington asked.

"That would be handy. She may be. That's not a bad way to dream death: simply don't." Madison commented.

"We commission all of these horror films to help our kids survive these steps, and we could just let them pass out?" Emerson wanted to know.

"Surely this has happened before," Salty said. The men quietly laughed. "She's just lying there. She looks like she is sleeping to me. Send someone in there." Salty was the group's doctor. "Wait. I'll go in."

Salty left the room. In a manner of minutes, Salty was in the room checking on Winter. He brought a pillow with him. He placed it under Winter's head, and he asked her if she was okay.

"I'm fine," she mumbled. Winter didn't actually yawn, but she adjusted to be more comfortable with the pillow.

Salty checked her pulse. "She's fine," he said and looked at the camera. Salty shrugged.

The men in the room Salty could not see stared back with blank stares.

Most apprentices see terrifying images and scream and pound the walls at least once for a few minutes. Not kidding. These are the psychologically and sometimes physically strongest beings on Earth. No one went to sleep. Winter's number was going up, and she was sleeping on the padded floor.

Salty Tweed returned to the switch room as it was called. "What's her number?"

"Twenty-nine." Madison ate a Red Vine.

"What is the time?" Salty asked.

"Eight a.m.," Madison said.

"She may be able to do all two hundred and twenty-two before five p.m.," Salty suggested. "The strongest persons I've seen prior to this were you, Madison, and Pete himself. Still. Both of you sat awake with your backs against the wall sweating for hours. This is unheard of."

"No," Washington said. "Winter Thompson reaches one hundred and eleven and rests for the remaining time until seven a.m. the next morning. We don't know what would happen if two hundred and twenty-two was reached on a girl in ten hours or less. It's been done with men but never with women. No."

Magellan turned to the seer stone. "Holy Guardian Angel, may I have audience?" A smoke angel symbol floated from the stone. "Can Winter Thompson handle two hundred and twenty-two deaths in ten hours?"

A green light showed up on all of the men's watches save Washginton's which remained blank because he disagreed but hadn't lied about it. Pete's newly obtained Omega lit up.

"Yes," rose from the stone.

Magellan gathered up the stone. "We're doing it. Sorry, Franklin. When she hits one hundred and eleven, let her sleep or whatever she wants to do," he said laughing, "for three hours, then run the rest before the immortal great conversations."

Chapter Sixteen
The Immortal Games: The Great Conversation, The Green Lights

Winter finished two hundred and twenty-two death dreams far before it was time for the Immortal Games.

No shots were fired Tuesday night. The immortals were so verbally and logically talented and clear – so honest with Carlos – the greatest conversations happened once a year in Las Vegas in October. Epictetus was quoted often. Examples of natural aristocracy and natural criminality were brought in from all over the world. In the "final round" on stage, seven men – one from each foundation – sat in a circle with shuffled pistols in a round theater and discussed whether or not a natural aristocracy existed. The pistols were never used, and as a sign of respect for each other, the pistols lay in a circle on a table in the center of the men. Franklin Washington spoke for The Plato Foundation. It was an important moment for St. Thomas School of Law as Notre Dame usually spoke for Plato. Were some men – regardless of their position in society when born – superior to others? The general consensus: no one knew. At the end of the night of amazing discussions, the men simply ran out of time: one hour and six minutes were allowed for each poker game. Green lights all around. Perfect English. Perfect participation. Perfect manners. Perfect logic. Perfectly honest. No perfect shots tonight. The last time a shot had been fired in the final round was two hundred years ago. Or so the rumor went. One did not lie to one's friends in Carlos Diaz's world.

Participants in rounds received money according to ability and level. Where the money came from, only Carlos Diaz knew, but the amounts were notable.

The final argument came from Franklin Washington: "Epictetus once said, death is only as we deem it to be. 'Thus, death is nothing terrible, else it would have appeared so to Socrates. But the terror consists of our notion of death, that it is terrible.' Natural aristocracy may be the ability to survive – we view ourselves as natural aristocrats because we belong to covenants of death which make us powerful. Who can determine who best survives? The poor? Woodcutters? Farmers? Nobility? Kings? Who best survives? To be a king is a heavy burden. Who is aristocratic? Who survives best? Perhaps no one knows."

At the end of the conversations, the audience applauded – Carlos Diaz entered the round and addressed the kings and audience consisting of apprentices, players, and immortal kings and king starlets: "Another successful beginning to the games. I declare the poker games free from the casinos and now afoot. As is said, watch your step. At stake this year are two U.S. Presidencies and a U.S. Supreme Court seat in addition to US2,000,000,000." The crowd applauded, and Carlos Dias turned to shake hands with standing players.

James Madison and Oscar Fouad participated in the Immortal Games for the first time tonight. Both were known throughout the country, and they received a standing ovation when they entered the arena stage for their past law instruction at St. Thomas School of Law. They were two of fourteen new kings. No women rose to King Starlets this year.

Madison and Fouad were matched against longtime immortals, and they held their own. Green lights only.

Winter Thompson looked amazing in her Versace. "Did you have any nightmares sleeping in a padded room, like in a scary movie?" Pete asked. They were sitting with the St. Thomas group rather than with their peers. Small groups of kings, players, and apprentices often formed throughout the United States. Men and women felt comfortable with this system. Pleased. Winter at this rate would be in the five hundred and fifty-five category sooner rather than later with her Henge Mage. This always happened at some point – and players loved to play. Skiing was a favorite of Pete Johnson, and he could not wait to risk it all on some of the most dangerous runs. There was no death squared consequence any more unless challenged by a higher up in his own organization while the game was on the ground. He could play with the big boys. He was excited.

"Yes. I had terrible dreams. Nightmares rarely affect me. Are you telling me I was supposed to be more terrified? Am I going to be pushed under water again?"

"Well…" Pete said. He sat there for about thirty seconds in astonishment. "Yes and no," Pete finally, exasperatedly said. "You won't be drowned again. But you have died two-hundred and twenty-two times this trip," Pete had given up not talking about her original death.

"Dean Anderson, do we have any tapes of Washington's experience?" Magellan wanted to know as the group stood up to go and eat after the final immortal conversation ended. The men laughed.

Franklin Washington turned. "Please, Magellan. My pride. Remember my pride." He smiled.

"No pride. We need Winter to understand how out of the ordinary she is. Let's call Elle," Magellan said.

All of the group went to Magellan's suite. A screen there was cued to a young Franklin Washington in a different padded room, in a casino, it appeared by the shots to the watchers. Washington sat in a corner in silent horror. He then stood and begged to be let out of the room. He pounded on the walls twice. "You can turn it off, Elle," Thomas Magellan said while my husband had stayed on the phone with me. "Professor Washington went through deaths which were different than yours – his were a bit more intense, but it is still notable that you *slept.*"

Richard Emerson ventured, "Tell us about your dreams if you don't mind, Ms. Thompson."

"I was continually being pushed over a ledge into a cement mixer. I would feel the crushing suffocation, and then I would feel a rush of adrenaline. This happened repeatedly in my dream until I lost count. I was able to count the number of times this happened until eleven. It was scary, but not terrifying. I've had terrifying dreams my whole life."

"Ah," Salty Tweed contributed. Some participants feel a great deal of adrenaline after death. Elle Magellan, sir, felt a lot of adrenaline, if I'm not mistaken?"

"That's correct. Elle – Winter, Elle is my wife – she gets a rush out of risk. As do you, we see. Magellan commented. He had not revealed to Winter he was the man in the bloodied-hand mask from her pool experience.

Winter asked, "Mr. Magellan, sir, who was the man who sent the game afoot and what does that mean? I couldn't quite see him. I could hear him."

"That's the Devil, my dear," Oliver Material answered for Magellan when Magellan indicated for him to do so. "The game's afoot means that players can shoot each other outside of the casino if engaged in conversation and if not clear or correct *at all* while the game is on the ground. Players keep track of each other's lights. They hunt each other if a player scores red. The players play to win until Christmas Eve. The teams with the highest kills and lowest deaths win a lot of money and rewards for their cohort. A common player phrase of old is 'Gaming until twenty-five December ; peace until October 1.' This has been changed to "Twenty-fifth ends the game, first ends the peace."

"Hm," Winter Thompson said. "Who are you people again? Why am I here?" She was serious. The men did not tease her.

"Pete?" Magellan indicated that the Henge Mage was to answer.

"Winter, your ancestors at some point made a deal with the Devil but have not been 'called in' for generations. You are bound to be with us. You belong with us. You actually have belonged to us since birth," Pete explained.

Winter smiled slightly. "You are frightening people. I'm not going to lie. You all are into some scary crap."

The men chuckled quietly. "Ms. Thompson," Cotton Anderson began, "what were your hopes in coming to law school? What did you hope to accomplish?"

"I thought I would become a school district's lawyer protecting teachers and administrators and then perhaps become a juvenile judge at some point."

"Those are great goals," Magellan stated. "Tonight, we

are going to request information from means we are all familiar with but you have not yet seen. You may be startled by what you see. You have no proof you have actually died – which you have – two hundred and twenty-two times since last week – and it is time we contact your group's Holy Guardian Angel to see if you will take the high road or the low road to fame. All players become famous in one way or another. These are the gifts of death to live: beauty, fame, wealth, power, and life for as long as you want it. Your body may shut down, but we can transfer you if you wish to stay here."

Winter's eyes widened. "I confess this is overwhelming. I sometimes wish I had never come to law school, that I was not part of this society."

"We know," Magellan kindly said. "We love you, Winter. Just know we are so glad you have joined us. We in the star network are in fact fated to this life. For most others, fate is a mythology, and they are right – for most others, fate *is* a mythology. For us, it must be. Carlos Diaz demands participation or curses untold reach out to our families for generations to come. We have become very civilized as a society in the world today. Some, in ancient times, gathered death numbers only through sacrifice of humans, not themselves or murder. We die ourselves nowadays. We are proud of our sacrifice to save the lives of innocents."

"I agree it could be worse," Winter said. "I'm so sorry if I insulted anyone."

"Not at all," Magellan said as he walked around the table in the living space of his suite. "Winter – may I call you by your first name?" He continued when she indicated of course, "I'm going to show you a stone. We in the star network use phones, but we also use stones to communicate. It's difficult to believe if you were not raised in our ways, but I want you to understand a little bit that you are in fact dying without literally seeing it even though you dream it, daily perhaps, until you reach five hundred and fifty-five deaths. We have staff who do the voodoo work. Your blood has already been gathered. You will get stronger, we normally say at this point, and you will be able to sit in class with ease while dying, but we think you might not be human."

The men quietly laughed again.

"You seem fine with death. Maybe it makes you sleepy, though? You will have to be able to die and still give speeches, take tests, have casual conversations, and more."

Magellan took his seer stone from his inside jacket pocket and placed it on the table. It was the same brown stone as before. "Holy Guardian Angel, are you present?"

A symbolic smoke angel in light floated from the stone. Winter Thompson was unmoved.

"Holy Guardian Angel, will Winter Thompson take the high road or the low road to beauty and fame?" Magellan asked.

"High road," the stone responded in letters floating from the stone, whole words at a time.

This is Elle. High road players died a lot. Low road players killed a lot. Pete was a low road player.

"How good of a shot is Winter among all new apprentices?"

"Last," said the stone.

Pete laughed out loud, then whispered, "I'm not going to lie, thank God. I thought if you could die with such grace and adrenaline and you were also a perfect shot, I was going to be outstripped soon by my own apprentice."

Magellan continued, "Holy Guardian Angel, will Winter kill and resurrect to become a Henge Mage when the time comes?"

"Yes." The stone shone.

Startled, Magellan picked up the stone. "Well. I confess Ms. Thompson, that although you are beautiful and have the grace of a goddess in death, I doubted you had what it took to finish this. We have a path called the 808 path which helps initiates who cannot compete as players to move into the world as workers throughout the country to help players. Your nurse was an 808. Our cleaners are 808s. I was fully prepared, I confess to all of you, to transition Winter to an 808 status right now. Pete, I see you're not surprised that I doubted her. But, it seems also you are not surprised that Winter can finish it. High road players rarely exist. You know this as well as I do. Pete, what do you predict the stone will say next?"

"Shot."

"Really?" Magellan looked incredulous.

He produced the stone again. Thomas was not ostentatious about using his seer stone. He simply was required by Carlos Diaz to put the stone away at *all* times when not used.

"Carlos Diaz, may we have audience?" The notable seven-point star appeared. "How will Winter Thompson be willing to kill before resurrecting her apprentice?"

"Shot," rose from the stone.

"Will she become a better shot?"

"No. Close range," rose from the stone.

"Shot was correct," Magellan indicated to Pete. "I stand corrected, Ms. Thompson. I apologize. Let's continue." Magellan addressed the stone. "Mr. Diaz, what's Winter

Thompson's song?" A smoky star rose from the stone. " 'Shook Me All Night Long' by AC/DC," rose from the stone.

Pete's head dropped.

"Sightless eyes are hers," rose from the stone.

The room was quiet. Then the men all laughed notably more loudly than they usually did. Still not loudly, but more loudly than normal.

"Winter," Salty Tweed said, "when you opened your eyes, did you see anything in the padded room?"

"No."

"That's right," Oscar Fouad commented. "Winter would have seen personal demons in the padded room – not in a dream."

"Carlos Diaz says she has sightless eyes," Oliver Material offered.

"Winter, do you have magical sight? Did you see anything coming from the stone?"

"I don't want to be rude, but I am unsure why we are staring at this stone. I have had no idea what you've been talking about for the last ten minutes."

Chapter Seventeen
Magically Blind

It was unsure whether or not a disabled magically blind player had ever been documented past Tiresias and a few Shakespearean witches.

Word spread quickly through Las Vegas as people boarded planes to return to various parts of the country. Everyone was returning home. A magically blind player. Rare. Would she believe the ways? She argued a lot so far, but Carlos Diaz had faith in her. Then they all did by contract. Still, some wondered if she would fare okay not understanding that magic confirmed the reality of their world. Some had seen her: she was a beauty for sure, but she would suffer, some believed. Many had then heard she didn't visualize the voodoo deaths the same way others did. But how would she handle being shot directly by her mentors and friends? Apprentices were busy preparing to "dream" when the first shots were fired. They themselves were not introduced to physical death again until five hundred and fifty-five even though they witnessed The Immortal Games. Most apprentices knew actual death (not death squared) in person followed five hundred and fifty-five – not just dreaming. The general consensus was that Winter Thompson had to believe that they were all nuts and she was stuck in a society of scary people with no morals.

But there were no magical sights previous to the stone

usage save demons, an Osiris member had argued as a group gathered in a conference room the next morning to discuss a blind player and eat breakfast.

Murmuring spread throughout the conference room. No one – and I mean no one – crossed Carlos Diaz. But Carlos Diaz was known to place people in locations to clear out players or kings with whom he was displeased. A blind dreamer or a Tiresias/ seer player brought about so many new factors to these cohorts in this generation that conferences were being formed to discuss the implications.

Players and kings officially in the game could not die squared unless taken out by a superior. Apprentices could not die squared until five hundred and fifty-five. It was the players between five hundred and fifty-five and six hundred and sixty-six who would be killing each other, dying, and living instantaneously. Eight-zero-eights could die squared. Innocents could die squared. A game of gotcha was about to go down between players, and Pete was preparing to be in class during the day and reading and running, as it was called, at night. Class was off-limits. Schools, for that matter, were off-limits during the day. To kill, one had to hit in the dark, not in public, or the deaths involved for both the hitter and the hit were subtracted from the hitter's count. And going public ensured loss. If any in your cohort ended up in the news for a crime, the game was up for that cohort.

Why play?

Well.

US political seats and a notable amount of money were at stake.

Carlos Diaz was not displeased with this current arrangement in the world where players died to strengthen players and innocents were mostly spared. Some argued that Mr. Diaz was softening in this generation. Magellan told all his cohort not to make such a mistake. "Carlos Diaz is dangerous. Do not forget it."

Terrorists killed innocents to run their death numbers up. The star network members in many parts of the world were not lying when they said they were noble. Carlos Diaz said that death was a part of life for leaders. It seemed so.

The St. Thomas Plato family sans Magellan who had been in the conference room with players across the US discussing Winter's situation and later on the phone with me in his suite had met in Winter and Pete's room.

Winter was embraced by the St. Thomas family with love, and the feeling among all of Plato was found to be mutual. Was she then a prophetess, was the next question? A witch? A medium?

Blind players in the past often could "see" or sense the future. "Not so," Winter laughed. "I would have been gone by the time Pete got to my house to take me to the 'party'."

"We would have known where you were, Winter," Pete pointed out to her. "Have you ever had a premonition that something was going to happen?"

"No."

"Have you ever seen spirits?" Material asked.

"Not to be rude, Professor Material, but how would I know? Wouldn't they look just like others?"

The men laughed. "No. Word is that they look ethereal. None of us are mediums. We don't actually know."

"What's her sixth sense, then?" Khalifa asked. He had been quiet the entire Vegas weekend.

"Kindness, I suspect," said Washington and winked at her.

"It will develop as she moves forward."

"Can we ask the stone?" Khalifa asked. "Is Mr. Magellan here?"

"Magellan is elsewhere, but Franklin and Mr. Emerson each obtained seer stones this weekend," Material offered. "I and Dean Anderson also have one," Material said.

"Winter, we see light coming from the seer stone we saw the other day and will from the stones we see today. The light forms images or words. You see nothing?"

"I promise, I see nothing." Her new watch lit green. Watches cleared good players or indicated that they were up for being shot for twenty-four hours if their red lights lit. The live watches meant they were in the thick of it by talking about this.

"When you said you could not see Carlos Diaz, did you mean you could not see him for the crowd, or you could not see him on the stage at all?" Oliver Material asked.

"I could not see anyone on the stage talking. No one on stage was talking, but I could hear the voice. Mr. Washington seemed to shake hands in the air symbolically."

"She cannot see Satan," Richard Emerson commented.

"He doesn't have a body. No one can *feel* his hand. But everyone can see it," Material continued.

"Winter, have you ever met the Devil?" Richard Emerson asked.

"No," Winter seemed startled.

"Pardon?" A tall man had entered the room to which Pete had left the door open to wait for Cotton Anderson who had run to check with Magellan about a few protocols.

"Excuse me, but most apprentices have met Carlos by now. My name is Al Thatch."

Everyone knew Al Thatch. Think of him as Bill Gates, but not noble. Al Thatch was with the Osiris Foundation but was not respected nor adored there anymore. Thatch was incredibly wealthy from a social networking site called Sinister and his company Five Connect had figured out how to create quadruple the energy from water power as well as being connected to oil. He was incredibly wealthy. Behind him came my husband, Cotton Anderson and Carlos Diaz., whom Winter could not see

Winter shook hands with Al Thatch, as did Franklin Washington. "She stays, Al," said Carlos Diaz. "Winter, can you see me?"

"I cannot."

"You obviously can hear me. Does this frighten you?"

"A little."

"I'm here. You do not have spiritual eyes, as religious people call it. We call it magical or finite material sight, the scientific term in our world. You are incredibly rare. You would not be able to feel me if we shook hands, but I will grab your hand. Place it out."

Winter outstretched her hand, and it moved up and down as the devil shook it. He could cause motion, but he could not be "felt" traditionally. But he was married to a human woman. Blonde. No one – and I mean no one – asked Lillith Diaz if she and the Devil were intimate. Some argued Carlos Diaz was above physical pleasures.

Winter said, "I felt my hand move up and down. I can see all of you. I just cannot see who is speaking. This is troubling."

Magellan entered the room.

Salty attempted to help her, "Ms. Thompson, you are a magical person who is disabled. You are spiritually blind, but not deaf. The fact that you can hear Mr. Diaz lets us know you fall into magical blood categories. You are just sightless or finite material disabled."

"Well," Carlos Diaz said. That settles that. "Has her gift been determined? I, of course, know what it is."

"It hasn't," Washington responded.

"No need for seer stones. I am here," Carlos began. "She hears the dead. It's different than a traditional medium. She has always heard the dead, but from what I can tell, she has always thought it was just people talking in another room or outside as she could not see anything attached to the sounds."

Winter looked panicked. She could perfectly hear Carlos speak, but from what I could tell, she could not see him at all. All other parties could see Carlos.

"Winter, do you hear any other voices you cannot see?" Pete asked.

Winter did not respond.

"Winter, we're sorry this is frightening. We need you to answer," Thomas, my husband said.

"Who is the woman, I can hear who seems to have come with Mr. Diaz and Mr. Thatch?"

"Shit," Oscar Fouad stood up. "I hate this truly scary shit. I'm up for death. I'm up for games. I'm up for getting shot and shooting others. I do not do ghosts. Hell. I'm not paid enough for this."

Madison laughed at Fouad.

"Winter, this is Carlos Diaz. I can see her. I can hear her. Tell Al Thatch what she said."

"She said, 'Mr. Thatch, I want my grave back.' "

Al Thatch did not flinch. Carlos Diaz turned to Mr. Thatch. "Al, I told you that you wouldn't regret the experience.

Winter Thompson is worth something to me. I could have told you the dead girl was there, but I wanted you to see for yourself what Winter can do."

"I'm satisfied. I'm out of here. Good luck, all of you." Thatch exited.

Carlos Diaz said to Pete Johnson, "Pete, stand next to Winter to give her comfort." Pete moved and placed his left hand on her right shoulder. "Winter," the Devil said, "I need you to learn how to hear the dead. I need you to be able to hear what others cannot hear. The dead comment in courts. I need you to advise the St. Thomas Plato lawyers about what you hear. The dead tell each other what they've seen, and they often give up the game."

"What will happen to the spirit who seems to have left with Mr. Thatch?" Winter asked Material.

Carlos Diaz responded, "Thatch will have an exorcist send her to heaven. Do not worry about her. Spirits are beyond spiritual eyes and ears. They can only be seen by mediums, witches, and sometimes prophets, if not blind. And me. You and Tiresias are similar: he also could hear but not see. He wasn't blind in his body – just like you. But the Greeks were unable to explain this to general audiences. Rest assured, the dead will find you."

Carlos Diaz was suddenly gone. He was not constrained by walls and doors.

"Why haven't I noticed this before?" Winter asked. "I guess I have only recently noticed extra conversations seemingly in another room or outside."

Salty Tweed responded, "Magic abilities and sight and sound generally only happen after initiation into black magic. Carlos seemed to imply she could hear the dead her whole life."

"I am overwhelmed, I confess," Winter stated.

This is Elle. It is of note that Winter's tone was becoming increasingly scared and less defiant.

"Pete?" Anderson asked.

"Winter, it must be scary to hear voices and know that we say we can see someone and you cannot. And it must be even scarier to hear a voice that the only being who confirmed you heard another voice we can't hear, was a being you cannot see but only hear." Pete tried to comfort Winter.

"I can't do this." Winter sat on the corner of the bed in her travel leggings and sweatshirt.

"You can." Pete kneeled near her. I, Elle, confess I was not unhappy about this development. Women often fell in love with their Henge Mages, and sometimes it worked: others, it didn't. With Thomas and I, it worked. I confess I wanted and want Winter and Pete to work out. Still, it was considered poor form to date before both were players.

"Winter, can you hear another voice or other voices in the room?" Salty looked concerned.

"I can't tell where they are, but someone keeps saying, 'Help me' since about a half hour ago."

"Address them," Salty suggested.

"Who needs help?" Winter asked.

"I do." The "lights" explained to me, Elle, what Winter was hearing.

"I can't see," Winter explained to the dead woman.

"I know."

"She said 'I know'." Winter asked again, "Are you connected to Mr. Al Thatch?"

"I'm not, I don't think. I actually don't know if I am," the ghost spoke kindly to Winter. Again, I could tell through the lights.

"She said 'I'm not'. What should I do? What do you want me to do? The ghost's voice actually clarified she isn't sure if she is connected to Mr. Thatch."

"Tell James Madison, 'The Jewish cemetery is in play,'" the spirit whispered.

Winter sighed. She had started to look vacantly forward as if she were physically blind, which she was not. "The voice, I'll call it, says to tell Mr. Madison whom she calls James Madison, 'The Jewish cemetery is in play'."

"I'm leaving Winter. There are spirits coming to talk to you. I would light a candle. Light a candle. Light a candle." The spirit seemed to chant a bit.

A tear rolled down Winter's face. "The voice said spirits are coming to talk to me and three times she said to light a candle."

"Lighting a candle gives mediums breaks. We'll contact room service." A knock on the door in three minutes indicated room service was aware of the room's activities. A concierge was there with twelve candles on a cart and a lighter. Their plane left in three hours.

Chapter Eighteen
Attraction

The men left Winter in Pete's hands. They did not make love albeit many people back at law school thought they did sometime during the Boston Marathon trip, as it was jokingly called. Winter was Pete's charge, and he felt the responsibility. The attraction was there. Even the respect.

They did kiss. But Pete ended with, "You're my apprentice. There are rules of dignity."

"Agreed," said Winter.

Winter went to sleep for an hour with the candles lit. Pete sat in a chair and read. He was wired.

Chapter Nineteen
Christmas Mass

The semester passed quickly. Winter dug into her studies as did Pete. Both found their academic rhythm by Halloween. The game was afoot, and Pete spent weekends skiing, rock climbing, and playing the equivalent of deadly paintball but with pistols. Conversations between players were always dictated by red-green Omega watch signals. People were tired. Only players played. Kings would have thrown the game by being able to take people out. Kings tried to throw the games often – but the key was to not get caught or lose. A player could not "kill squared" another player. A king could, so kings rarely shot, but could throw the game in other ways by making life difficult for a player and being paid to do so. Players could shoot and kill which would add five kills to their score and one death to the score of the hit. The goal was to kill and not die, but dying also benefited the players. It was the perfect game where sacrifices for Carlos Diaz were contained mostly within the system, granting power to those who risked and leaving the innocent free from terror unlike ancient days of war and human sacrifice. This was a beautiful but difficult time of year for the star network's players. The time leading up to Christmas midnight was filled with elongated player deaths. *Physical deaths* and instant regenerations without incantations for five hundred and fifty-five and above took energy. Pete was eating more than he had eaten his entire life.

Winter could suffer – as far as they could tell – one slower voodoo death a week. The work of the technicians were similar. With a vial of blood on a Venus statue named Winter Thompson, they could behead the statue, and Winter would scientifically have died in the same manner. Thomas speculated Winter could suffer two or three a week making her a player in time shorter than usually required. Still, at one a week, Winter was mentally strong, sleeping well, and in good spirits. She'd "dream" the type of death she was experiencing, but no unnatural amount of fear was felt. "Just a daydream to Winter," became a saying among players at St. Thomas School of Law.

Pete and Winter almost held hands as they ran through the snowy night toward the law school from the bar (Winter still did not drink, but Pete loved a half glass of whiskey on a holiday night, and everyone thought the game was over – most players avoided drinking during it, but immortals could do what they wanted and it didn't faze them) down the street. Law students were pouring into the school for the mass. Professors wandered down from their offices because Cotton Anderson had asked that professors check in at eleven whereas the game was supposed to be over at midnight. The winning foundation would be declared tomorrow. Washington and Emerson had come earlier than that for a special occasion discussed later. Pete was at death five hundred and seventy-one. Ten kill deaths (two kills he inflicted on other players during night runs – the players lived whereas they were in the game) ,five sport deaths (skiing), and his death on the roof of the Bellagio. Pete ended up being rather adept at dangerous sport. Five deaths was nothing for a five hundred and fifty-five where these emerging immortals skied.

In first place as the best scoring new player in the star network, Pete was celebrated by his acquaintances from other foundations as he walked into the law school to attend mass. Winter wore her overstuffed North Face coat – white – and a pink beanie hat. Star network members knew to explain magical information they had received to Winter. Winter was adjusting to believing what she could not see. She had a candle or two or three lit in her apartment at all times. She wasn't ready to embrace her talent of hearing the dead.

The dead did follow her to school though. "Professor Washington, did you know there is a spirit which stands, I think, at the front of the room with you and repeats everything you say? It's annoying but useful," she had once said to Franklin Washington. Professors started lighting a small candle behind their podiums. No need for a dead peanut gallery everyone agreed.

Elle here. Many people think candles call spirits to them. Not so. Lack of natural light – darkness – calls spirits. Fluorescent or electric lights are also comfortable for the dead, Winter has since explained to me a spirit explained to her. Natural light, outside buildings or with fire in a building nearby at least one hundred feet near, made the dead very uncomfortable. The spirit explaining this to her said it makes spirits so uncomfortable – fire and sunlight – that they avoid both at all costs. The spirit explained that the only comfortable place in St. Thomas School of Law classrooms was near the podium away from the natural light windows. The dead avoid me, Elle Magellan.

Mediums are incredibly rare. Blind mediums come once in a

thousand years or so. The Plato Foundation felt honored Winter had committed to the group. Winter's Omega watch was with Thomas Magellan when he administrated over what is called the resurrection night: when she came back to life, the watch shone green. She would be good to the organization. She would be loyal. She just didn't know it herself.

Deaths became more difficult the further one went up in number of deaths. Voodoo deaths usually were quite bearable for the first two hundred and twenty-two. For some reason, two hundred and twenty-three brought about madness, depression, angst, and more at a lengthened time rather than in short spurts as was not the case up to two hundred and twenty-two, and the speed of administering the deaths had to be slowed to a three-year process to get someone to five hundred and fifty-five. No one knew how Winter would handle the slower voodoo deaths as the deaths between two hundred and twenty-three and five hundred and fifty-five were slower and more difficult to psychologically take. Many predicted she would again be more than fine.

Seer stones could project visions which could be converted to a screen-like situation. A space can be designated a "screen" and a two-dimensional image projects to the space as requested using an incantation. These could then be filmed. Many didn't know Stonehenge was a large outdoor viewing room for war. The stones create viewing windows like on a computer. The stones themselves are very large seer stones unused for centuries. I suspect they still work, but the space is now too public. All of my story so far has been mostly through cameras, save for a few thought processes by the people involved about which I asked a small stone what was being thought by them at the time.

Thomas had looked around and found Winter Thompson a singing stone. These were incredibly rare for apprentices to own because: a) they were not kings or king starlets and b) they were notably expensive and required a great deal of belief to operate. Singing stones were not in high demand as they were not as useful to the average black magic mage simply because seer stones gave visuals and singing stones only verbally explained things, and often in riddles. Still, the singing stones spoke truths as requested, and it was brought to Magellan and me, both who had stayed in the Minneapolis area through Christmas and New Year's Day. I can watch anyone from anywhere if the subjects are party to The Plato Foundation, but St. Thomas is home. The law school is relatively young. Thomas, my husband, and I are Tommies – University of St. Thomas undergraduates – and Notre Dame law graduates.

Thomas had wrapped the singing stone in a small gift box and had given it to Pete to give to Winter. Seeing stones that gave both sight and sound were quite large. I used Thomas's Henge Stone as sound and sight stones were called, and we kept it with us, but it had to be moved by car or private plane from location to location. It weighed 136 kilograms Thomas carried around a sight stone.

It was eleven thirty p.m., twenty-four December 2028. The crowd was filling in. There would not be enough room for the entire law school in the chapel, but some had not risked the surprisingly mild cold to participate. All players and apprentices were present though. It was exciting. To belong. To belong to an ancient society which made a difference and was full of tradition and financial safety. It felt good. Winter was delighted this Christmas night, adjusting to her new reality.

Thomas took Winter and Pete to Anderson's office, and they placed the singing stone on the table. "Ask it a question."

"Do I ask to talk to the Holy Guardian Angel or Carlos Diaz?"

"Not Carlos Diaz." The men laughed. "No, no, no. Just ask to speak to a Holy Guardian Angel. One attends all seer and singing stones."

"Holy Guardian Angel," Winter began, "may I approach?"

"Dance with me, Winter, and hear," the stone responded.

Winter's jaw dropped. She could hear it. "Could you hear that?" she asked. Pete, Thomas, and Cotton laughed. I confess I, Elle, am getting more personally involved in this history, but it's journaling of the most basic kind. I am now sometimes referring to my husband by his first name and friends by theirs as well. I'll try to refer to them as Magellan and Anderson again going forward. Hopefully.

"How many deaths have I suffered since Las Vegas?" Winter asked.

The stone "spoke" in a sing-song voice "What is two hundred and thirty-three minus one?"

Through Dean Anderson's office door, Madison, Fouad, and Washington walked in.

"Ah," Washington said. "Winter's singing stone. Great job on a successful first gaming era and receiving an important gift. Also, I was impressed with your Constitution Law paper. Fine job."

"It is packed down there." Fouad laughed. "I mean, there is a group of over two hundred."

"I'm going to go see what's up at the Jewish cemetery,"

Madison said. Remember, Magellan had charged the men not to tell Winter her DNA Jewish heritage which could not be traced merely through genealogical research without secret records. Mormons were genealogical experts, and DNA services abound, but DNA did not always match up with location. "We want to see why the Jewish cemetery is in play. We're going to skip out on mass. We promise to say a thank you prayer in the car."

"We understand. If the dead say go and see, best do it," Anderson said.

"Best do it," Madison said with another Red Vine in his mouth.

"I'll come," Fouad said.

"Wait, you two. I'll come too," Washington said.

All three men took the stairs and not the elevator. The crowd in the foyer was excited and happy. Christmas music was playing on the speakers in the hallways and open spaces. "White Christmas" by Bing Crosby played out into the open space. The drive to the cemetery went quickly. The men stood on a frozen mound looking at upturned graves.

Franklin Washington was crouching near the ground and played with the dirt with his hands. "A local cemetery owner sold this part of the cemetery to billionaire Al Thatch. The graves are all over one hundred years old and have few relatives around to protest. Still. Feels spiritually dangerous," Franklin Washington's toothpick moved around his mouth in a methodical motion.

"You superstitious, Washington?" Madison asked.

"Not going to say I'm not. Digging up the dead – especially notably old dead – isn't sport, friend, as you remember from our Las Vegas trip." Washington laughed softly. "I wouldn't have done this. Yes. A bit superstitious."

A fluttering of wings startled the air. "Damn." Fouad turned around to see a great blue heron fly away.

"Don't curse in a cemetery," Washington requested.

Madison laughed.

Fouad responded, "Seriously, Washington, you are making me feel like a Dickens ghost is going to come around a tomb. Let's get out of here."

"Come on, Franklin." Madison lightly pulled Washington's overcoat. Washington stood up.

Franklin Washington and Oscar Fouad first descended the small frozen hill. James Madison stood there for a bit and said, "This is not going to end well. But this has not been in play in the past few months. I don't understand the dead, it appears."

The men got into Madison's car – Fouad in the back – and they drove through the city. The radio notified the men a big storm was coming to the city in the next twenty-four hours. News stations had predicted there would be a power outage because of the amount of snow expected: electricity lines were just not expected to be able to handle the weather. "Let's head to my house. You boys stay with me," Washington said to the men who were thirty-three and older, but to him, they were kids.

When they reached Washington's home, they found that Emerson had already let himself in. The four of them decided to read Dickens aloud and have a glass of whiskey with a very late dinner. Washington had a housekeeper, a woman by the name of Ms. Taylor.

They spent the day celebrating the end of death for another year – time to work in the trenches of law and politics – when the storm hit. The winds were far fiercer than predicted. The power was out by five p.m. Christmas Day.

The next night, twenty-six December 2028, Washington said, "Let's go to the law school and discuss with Anderson, if he's there, why the dead would warn Madison the cemetery was in play. Nothing happened. Nothing happened with the cemetery."

A few hours later, after standing over a dead body in the foyer of the law school, Anderson said, "I'm not kidding. If I later find out any of you had a hit out on this guy and the player did it in front of the law school to let you know the job was done, I'm going to f— you up before I forgive any of you."

"Clear," Washington said. A green light appeared on Washington's watch.

"Clear," Emerson said. Green.

"Clear," Madison said. Green.

"Clear," Fouad said. Green.

Cotton Anderson looked down where his absent watch would have shown red.

"Thank God," Anderson replied. Red and blue lights appeared through the windows. Men with a stretcher came through the door.

Madison pointed out a small tattoo – an 808 – on the deceased's wrist, but it looked like two infinity signs with an opal between. "He's with us?"

"Not sure," Washington responded.

"Wait," Cotton Anderson said. "I had him killed. I forgot."

All of the men looked over at Cotton.

Pounding on the door resulted in Oscar Fouad and James Madison opening the doors to the paramedics who soon declared the man dead and took the body away.

"We'll clean," Cotton Anderson responded to some men

who asked him some questions.

"Poor janitorial staff," the police officer laughed as he closed the door behind him – the last official to leave.

"Yes, poor janitorial staff, Cotton," Emerson was now yelling. "You dueled us. Pay us. You scared the shit out of me asking me to declare myself clear, Cotton. Explain yourself."

"For my mistake, US$10,000 is already in each of your accounts." Cotton Anderson headed toward the elevators. "Follow me. I have a lot going on right now, and I can't afford to have anyone beneath me doing deals without letting me know. It's worth a mere forty thousand to see who is still clear. I'm not. Shit. I can't believe my player killed him in the front yard. Good God. Sorry, Emerson. You know this as well as I do: a game is a game."

"Cotton, the game was supposed to end two nights ago, . Christmas Eve, 2028 – the scrolls all said it." Fouad implied his question.

Washington's countenance darkened. "Do you mean to tell me the game is still on the ground"

All five men were crammed into the elevator now. It was silent save for Harry Styles singing "Hey Jude".

A bell sounded.

"Yes." Cotton sighed. "But you know I love it."

"What in the hell happened?" Emerson yelled. "Why is the game still afoot? My God, what if that body is traced back to you, Cotton? It was in the snow outside the law school."

"It won't be."

"It might be linked to someone here. The body was *shot*."

"I know the police chief. He's with us. It won't get to that because it was me. If it would have been any of you, it could have come to the news. It won't. I thought maybe you knew the game was still on." Cotton Anderson opened his office's secretary's space. They all walked in in the dark. The lights sputtered and then went on as electricity returned to the city

Beaming light filled the foyer. The blood on the floor was being cleaned by men in janitorial outfits. Again, I, Elle, will note Madison smiled to himself. He had complete faith in this system.

The phone in Anderson's office rang. All of the men entered as Cotton picked up the phone. "Yes?" Laughter. "Yes. It was unfortunate that a victim nearby, was hurt and walked here, don't you agree, Chief?" Cotton looked down. "I'm here working on the Epictetus Dilemma. I would hate for this to be in the papers." Madison took a seat. "Great. I'm glad to hear it." Anderson held the landline as he picked up his cell phone, sent a text after writing, "Now kill the killer and blame him."

"What is going on, Anderson?" Emerson grabbed the landline phone from Anderson and slammed it down on the base. "Plato hasn't killed an innocent in over two hundred years. Explain yourself."

"No one's innocent."

The room was incredibly tense. At my house where I was watching the law school scene, Magellan walked into my writing room and demanded I turn off the screens for twenty minutes. He then left the room. I set a timer. When I resumed the screens, the men were each camped out in their respective offices for the night. The storm was resuming.

Chapter Twenty
Call to Adventure

I, Elle, am now going to cut to the day after Christmas at Winter's apartment before the power was restored

Winter sat in her apartment with candles lit in every room. Pete practically lived there. Khalifa too. Pete and Winter slept platonically in her bed and Khalifa slept on the couch. Her landlord didn't care as the apartments were owned by Washington. Winter had familiarized herself with the Holy Guardian Angel associated with this singing stone. Dark angels do not fear natural light: the dead do. Few know the many differences between angels and the dead. I don't, anyway. Not yet. Thomas may. One does not always have to ask permission to approach a singing stone. One simply asks. If the angel is nearby, she or he will answer. Winter's Holy Guardian Angel was always around it seemed. She seemed to like Winter. Everyone liked Winter.

Winter had not asked her stone about the cemetery because the dead had directed the comment to her superior: James Madison. Henge Mages are not always about-to-be newly minted players. Sometimes if a great player was predicted, immortals were used to be Henge Mages as was the case with James Madison whose Henge Mage was Cotton Anderson who was already immortal when he initiated Madison.

Khalifa was making a roast in the kitchen using a crock pot using a generator. He was peeling and chopping carrots. Pete was on the couch typing on his previously fully charged computer. Winter was lying on her bed rolling the singing stone around with her hand. She playfully decided to address the Holy Guardian Angel. "HGA, may I approach?" she asked. The pine candles flickered in her room this winter night with no power.

"Yes. Yes. Yes," said a singing voice, lighthearted and beautifully kind.

"Am I allowed to ask about the cemetery?"

"Yes. Yes. Yes," sang the voice. "I have been waiting for you to be ready to ask.

"What does it mean that the cemetery is in play?"

"What does it mean to be in play? In play? In play in a casino? One asks," sang the stone.

"Does 'In play' mean the cemetery has leverage in the game? It's worth money to someone?"

"More. More. More. More."

"It means the cemetery causes more deaths?"

"Closer. Closer. Closer. What guards the rivers and stops the heroes if it can?"

"I don't know, Holy Guardian Angel."

"You will. You will. You will. Goodnight, sweet girl."

Winter was asleep by four-thirty p.m. On December 26, 2028.

When Winter awoke, Khalifa was sleeping on the floor on his bedding in Winter's room and Pete had fallen asleep on his now dead computer on the couch with a blanket that had been over the back of the couch around him. It was eight a.m., and the lights in the kitchen were on from when the power had gone off; power was restored to the city. It was December 27, 2028, and the law students were on holiday. She knelt next to Pete: "Pete. Pete." Pete opened his eyes.

"The Holy Guardian Angel asked me, 'What guards the rivers and stops the heroes if it can?' "

Pete sat straight up. Khalifa came running out of her room. "What did you say?" Khalifa asked.

Confused, Winter said again, "The HGA asked me what guards rivers and stops heroes if it can?"

"My God," whispered Pete. "You're ahead of us. The answer to that question is 'threshold guardian'. Winter, are you already immortal?"

Khalifa knelt next to Winter. "Winter, Pete's serious. The hero's journey is only put-upon immortals. Men and women like professors Franklin Washington and Richard Emerson start their hero's journey in their forties. Did you receive a call to adventure? It's how kings are fully seated. One has to be a king, lose it all, and then become a king on safer ground again. Professors Washington and Emerson had a very difficult road behind them, but they are finished, they received their seer stones, and their true wills will come to pass. Washington is supposedly a US Presidential candidate before this is all over for him. He is predicted to win by the stones if we win The Epictetus Dilemma.

"Maybe she's an 808 and the Holy Guardian Angel is redirecting her," Pete suggested, "although, I doubt it. Something is astonishing about this."

Pete made a phone call while Khalifa got Winter to eat. Soon, Magellan, Washington, Emerson, Tweed, Material, Madison, and Fouad joined the three young Plato Foundation members. They all crammed into Winter's apartment. Pete explained to the men what Winter had said.

I, Elle, would like to comment here on the Emirati stance on Israel. The Arabic nation of the United Arab Emirates did not always recognize Israel as a sovereign nation, but they were not unsympathetic to the human story. Khalifa loved Winter. Winter still didn't even realize she was genetically Jewish.

"Winter," Magellan began, "this is important. Have you ever thought you have died before at someone's hand?"

"Yes. When I was eleven, I went to spend the summer with some friends my parents trusted. I fell forty-eight feet from a cliff where we were camping. I had been hiking with our group. I felt that I had died. Apparently a hiker passed me on the lower switchback and I woke up to him saying words I could not understand." Winter looked concerned. Her attitude was completely checked at this point. She had finally embraced her new life.

"My family and I have always thought he was just confusing to me because I didn't know him, and he was speaking a foreign language to me as a child. We assumed he had been speaking Arabic, and that I had just not understood. He spoke English to the paramedics. I was lucid by the time the paramedics reached me. I had a broken ankle and right arm," Winter continued.

"Did you ever see the man again?" Magellan asked Winter. "Winter, this is important."

"Yes. He ended up being my ski instructor. He worked the trails during summers. That's how I was able to learn about where he was from and what languages he spoke. Do you think I've been killed and resurrected before?"

"Winter," said Magellan, "Yes. This is important. Can you

remember your ski instructor's name?"

"Yes. Hamdam Allah."

"We need to contact him. Do you think he would still be in Utah?" Magellan pressed.

"No. He died in a skiing accident when I was in my second year of ski lessons. I was thirteen. He taught me and all of the kids of my friend's family. We connected to him when he helped me with what we thought were only broken bones on the trail – not a resurrection of sorts."

"Had you ever met him before?"

"No." Winter thought for a minute. "We could ask the singing stone."

"Good idea, Ms. Winter," Washington stated. "Let's ask your Holy Guardian Angel."

Magellan sort of whispered to himself, "I wondered why I was cleared to give her a stone. We had heard it was rare for a person this young to obtain a stone, but if she is at the point where one receives a stone, that is different.

"Winter, have you received a call to adventure?" Magellan asked.

"I don't think so. Should we ask the HGA?" Winter asked.

No one corrected Winter when she informally referred to Holy Guardian Angels as HGAs. Her magical blindness caused one to forgive her lack of usually desired formalities.

"Let's," Magellan agreed.

"HGA, may I have audience?" Winter asked.

The stone sang, "Of course, sweet girl. Of course, sweet swirl."

"Holy Guardian Angel, am I immortal?"

"Are you?" sang the stone. "What do you think?"

"May I ask it a question?" Magellan asked Winter.

"Of course."

"Sweet Holy Guardian Angel of Winter Thompson's, will you show yourself to those of us who can see dark angels but not the dead?"

Winter backed up from the floor next to the couch and crawled into Pete's arms.

"Agreed. This will help," sang the stone. "I shall disperse with singing, if you don't mind. Remember, red-light, green-light does not work with me – with any holy guardian angel."

"Do candles make a difference?" Winter asked.

"No," Pete explained. "Dark angels (Holy Guardian Angels) and demons are different from the dead. Neither dark angels nor demons were ever people with bodies on Earth. Dark angels and demons are immortal by nature like Carlos Diaz and their bodies cannot be felt by humans, dreamers, players, unseated kings, or immortals who were once human. . We can see and hear the devil, dark angels, and demons. The 'average' black magic mage can see and hear dark angels and demons but not the dead. Non-disabled mediums, I have read since I met you, can see and hear everything: the devil, dark angels, demons, and the dead. You just can't see them because you are a blind medium. "

The stone spoke, "I love natural light, Winter. I love natural light."

Light filled the room.

"Winter," Pete asked, "Can you see that?"

"See what?"

An angel with wings appeared and bowed to the room. Her bare feet were about three yards above the floor. She was wearing a gown of gold, and her black and white wings moved beautifully. "She cannot see me, gentlemen. Can you hear me, Winter?"

"I can hear you," Winter said. "What do you look like?"

"I look a lot like Penelope Cruz, actually." The men quietly laughed. "I'm not her, of course, but that is my general appearance. I have black and white wings, and I'm in the air. Do you know the actress Penelope Cruz?"

"I do."

"I normally would not make such a comparison, but you cannot see. I have a call to adventure for you, Winter. Do you know the answer to my question – my riddle? What guards the rivers and stops the heroes if it can?"

"A threshold guardian, these two friends told me is the answer."

"That is correct. You will be blessed with true friends your entire life," the Holy Guardian Angel said.

"Winter, I'm here to tell you that you are already partially immortal. Drowning takes resurrection incantations even for immortals, but you would have lived anyway. Shots are the easiest to recover from. You were made partially immortal by a coalition of Middle Eastern peace bearers called The Red Horse who have been watching you since birth. Your name showed up in a stone in Dubai when you were ten. It is still unclear whether or not your immortality will hold whereas you have not initiated another apprentice, have not been shot at five hundred and fifty-five, nor have you yet completed your hero's journey to be a seated king starlet. But your death count is well over two thousand," The Holy Guardian explained.

"You need to complete the hero's journey to be safe. I am also your threshold guardian, and you will walk past me – you cannot even see me – some will argue you did not do this step because you will not be able to recant what happened. The men here are all witnesses that you will pass the threshold guardian – me – but they will never be able to tell you what they see when you do it. It is forbidden. Your historian can write parts. Do you know you have a historian?"

"I do not."

No one – not even Thomas Magellan – contradicts a Holy Guardian Angel's decision to share information. Carlos Diaz had given us strict instructions to never tell Winter Thompson about her historian: me. We never did. But Holy Guardian Angels were in contact with Carlos Diaz. Surely, things were okay?

"Winter, you must never mention nor ask about your historian past this point."

"I understand."

"Would you like to go on an adventure? There are those in the USA cohorts who want to start a war to switch death quotas from being obtained by dying ourselves to innocents dying for us in a war in the middle East. Al Thatch refuses to die himself any more. I call you, and your two friends, to help with Middle Eastern peace by avoiding network civil war here in the U.S. Do you accept?"

"I do."

The HGA – I'll playfully call her since now I felt endeared to Winter beyond words knowing that dark angels knew I was watching her story – flew in front of the door to the hallway. "Winter, just walk out the door. If you are pure in heart, I'll move. If you are not, I cannot tell you what happens next. Franklin Washington and Richard Emerson both passed this test years ago. Mr. Magellan, Mr. Tweed, Mr. Materials, and Mr. Anderson passed even more years past. They are seated kings. We don't just kill off great people. Do not fear death. Only fear being cut out of the great conversation."

Winter didn't hesitate. She stood up and walked out the door. I, Elle, can't fully explain what happened. Winter walked toward the door being blocked by the angel's left wing. The wing moved, and the angel covered her face with the wing opening the way to the door. Winter walked outside and closed the door. The angel then did something I am not allowed to write. She then disappeared.

Magellan opened the door to Winter who entered.

"Oh. My. God. You're an unseated King Starlet," Khalifa said.

The men laughed, not so loudly, and quietly applauded for her.

"Winter," said Magellan. "The hero's journey is incredibly dangerous. In ancient times, players went through the hero's journey at a young age. As we have advanced, it has been deemed ungentlemanly to make players suffer as much as is needed in The Hero's Journey as it was deemed by Joseph Campbell. Immortals past six hundred and sixty-six do it better. They suffer less."

As we all realized at this moment that Winter was past six hundred and sixty-six in deaths, we realized this which why the nightmares were not terrifying for her as would have been when she was younger. "She's past six hundred and sixty-six already," Pete whispered, "but she has not yet killed and resurrected someone nor completed her hero's journey."

An unearthly light filled the room again and all but Winter could see. Pete explained. Winter's Holy Guardian Angel appeared again. "I have terrifying news," she said.

"I must offer a call of adventure to Pete and Khalifa because they answered the threshold guardian question for Winter. Even though they are players only, Carlos Diaz demands they go through the door right now."

Pete and Khalifa stood up.

"Men, Peter Johnson and Khalifa Abdul Mohammed, I

call you to the same call to adventure: you will help usher in Middle Eastern peace. Winter You must pass through my block through the door together and you will be bound together forever. Khalifa will never kill. He is the high road. Pete must kill. He is the low road. Together they will work with Winter to make a difference.

"I do," the twenty-three-year-old boys said in unison.

"Walk through if you dare. Pete first. If either is not pure, I will drop my wing and block him."

Both boys approached the door, and the Holy Guardian Angel lifted her wing and blocked her view while the boys both went through the door. Pete first, Khalifa second. Both boys closed the door. Again, the Holy Guardian Angel had an additional step she did twice which I am not allowed to write here. She explained to me what not to include by addressing me directly but not by name. She called me "historian" likely because Winter was present.

"Open the door." As the door opened, the HGA disappeared for a moment. When the door closed, as the boys sat on the couch next to Winter, the HGA reappeared and repeated her message now explaining that because James Madison and Oscar Fouad had witnessed this experience, they also were called to the same adventure after answering the riddle. Both men were clear when asked to leave the room and re-enter.

"Well," said the Holy Guardian Angel. "My name is Xipe-Totec, and I answer to all stones from this group. The singing stone belongs to Winter, and she is the prophetess for Pete and Khalifa. Khalifa, I'm afraid your family will not be able to alter your path at this point, but I know the sheikhs in Dubai and Abu Dhabi are familiar with your story. Your path is clear to move forward. You will stay here and finish law school before going to medical school. I will reveal now that Washington and Emerson were called to help with Middle East peace years ago. We, the dark angels on high, now call the remaining seated kings here: Thomas Magellan, Cotton Anderson, Oliver Material, and Alistair Tweed to help with this journey. Winter, why don't you ask your friends how they knew the answer to this game's threshold guardian question? I know, of course, naughty boys."

"Isn't the answer always 'threshold guardian'?" Winter's seeming impertinence was forgiven her instantly because she was magically blind and now so incredibly sweet. She had done a 180 from defiance and anger to compliance and buy-in that charmed everyone who saw her.

"It's not," replied the HGA.

"How did you know the answer?" Winter asked.

Pete and Khalifa stood up. Pete responded, "We confess we used your stone when you were asleep. We asked Xipe-Totec, your Holy Guardian Angel, some questions. We asked what had passed for Professors Washington and Emerson. We weren't trying to be dishonest. We knew Winter wouldn't care. It's fun to know something new."

"Carlos Diaz saw." The Holy Guardian Angel turned her head away and covered her face with her wings. When she uncovered her face, she had streaming tears. "I am required to answer if a pure heart asks. Two pure hearts could not be denied. Carlos Diaz demands they start their hero's journeys before full immortality and before being immortal."

"Yes," said Magellan. The men were all silent. All five – James Madison, Oscar Fouad, Pete Johnson, Khalifa Mohammed, and Winter Thompson – were in too deep, but particularly Pete and Khalifa who would have to go through the Road of Trials as it was known without any type of immortality. Unseated kings and king starlets sometimes died squared during the Road of Trials and the Magic Flight.

The HGA continued, "The only other person who will know this call will be your historian. Please do not share your knowledge or face the consequences, Carlos Diaz, the god of this world, says. And," she bowed her head, "all heroes and kings know, dark angels believe in a different God, and Carlos Diaz cannot force us to talk differently about the kindest being in the universe. Carlos Diaz is the God of this World, the Eternal God of War, as I call him, for now. But may the God of the universe be with you all."

She disappeared.

Chapter Twenty-One
Star Network

The three youngest St. Thomas Plato family members, I'll now call them, all started to speak at once.

Winter sat in shock. "Who gives calls? Carlos Diaz? The man I could only hear and not see? Is he really the devil?"

Pete questioned his sanity, "Am I still asleep?"

Khalifa knew this was real. "Can dark angels contradict Carlos Diaz? I did not know that. Are we in trouble?"

"It's very secret, Khalifa," Magellan whispered. "Some dark angels are at war with the devil. It's not new."

Fouad stood up, "You mean to tell me we have a Holy Guardian Angel who is at war with the devil? I'm not going to lie. This terrifies me."

"Carlos will likely not cross a dark angel. Do not worry. As for us, we render unto Caesar that which is Caesar's. Carlos Diaz is the God of this World. We obey him, but we also obey our Holy Guardian Angel. Holy Guardian Dark angels also render unto Carlos that which is Carlos's – on occasion, they try to circumvent Diaz. Diaz knows he has unruly subjects. Carlos doesn't want or even need to be loved. Carlos wants to be all-powerful, and is," Magellan tried to comfort the group.

"Is he angry at Khalifa and myself? He punished us for using the singing stone without permission," Pete directly addressed Thomas Magellan.

"I don't know. Let's ask my stone." Magellan produced his stone, notably different from Winter's, and laid it on an oversized mismatched ottoman.

"Carlos Diaz? May we have audience?" Nothing happened.

"I cannot ask Carlos Diaz for audience twice in one effort. Holy Guardian Angel? My Holy Guardian Angel is different from yours. Or was. I'm unsure what will happen."

A smoky angel symbol of light appeared from the stone. Pete explained to Winter that she or he was answering. "Do Peter Johnson and Khalifa Abdul Mohammed need to apologize to Carlos Diaz?"

Nothing happened. Then a star appeared.

The words streamed from the stone:

"A World War is coming starting in the Middle East," shown on the wall in red and orange fire lettering.

The writing continued. "You all have consorted with an enemy dark angel. Pete and Khalifa have used a stone without permission. How, I want to know, did Peter Johnson and Khalifa Abdul Mohammed pass the threshold when they had been untrue?" The writing was from Carlos Diaz. It was explained to Winter.

Oliver Material gasped. "The holy guardian angel must have let them pass. Watches do not work with dark angels."

"I thought I was dead," Khalifa said.

"I knew we'd make it," Pete said.

"It's not possible. No angel can defy science. The boys must have been pure in some way," Magellan said. "No offense, Material, but Dark Angels are also bound by the God of this World and by science. Carlos Diaz knows that. Carlos must have not commanded the angel fully, leaving it a window.

The angel has crossed Carlos Diaz. She'll be dead by tonight in the way immortals die. She's probably already dead," Anderson added to the conversation.

"Dark angels can die?" Winter asked.

"Dark angels can die," Magellan said. "Now I know Diaz's feelings, my prediction is that our stones will cease to work soon. We will be cut off from the star network, but we have all already passed into the hero archetype. This is going to get brutal. I have savings."

"I have savings." Emerson also said.

"We all do, except these kids. I own this apartment," Washington offered.

"I don't understand. We're no longer part of The Plato Foundation?" Pete asked incredulously.

"That is what this means," Material said.

"Anderson, you had an eight-o-eight killed last night. Why? I was confused. How is the game still afoot? Eight-o-eights sometimes defect. Why did you kill him?" Magellan asked.

"Carlos Diaz visited me earlier yesterday and offered me clemency since I have not been part of this story in the way which all of you have: Diaz wanted Washington killed. I responded by having the assassin sent by Carlos Diaz to kill Washington killed. I was still connected enough to have it done. Diaz will realize it soon. He will not be happy. None of you were ready to hear I had been treasonous. You all trusted I would never be so. I would," Anderson offered.

"I don't understand. None of this had happened last night. Why would Carlos Diaz send someone to kill the star network's revered Franklin Washington?" Madison asked.

Madison looked more panic-stricken than he had ever

looked to anyone. I cannot tell you his thoughts because my stone had ceased to work. As of this point, I still had camera access. But I can guess James Madison was devastated at the failing of the system. "Just don't additionally consort with the Devil," he had told me his father had told him. "You'll be fine. Our system is good," his father had told him, Madison once explained to me.

"My dad has told me the system is always good," Madison offered.

"No, it's not always good," Magellan corrected. "If it were always good, atrocities would not happen in the United States."

"How would an eight-o-eight be able to kill an immortal?" Winter asked.

"Carlos asked me to "lend" the eight-o-eight some of my power thinking I was more loyal to Carlos than to Washington," Anderson responded. "Before the borrower was able to harness my power, I had my guy kill him."

"Lending means that for a split second, the assassin or protected borrows immortality taking it for that same amount of time needed to either kill or live. It's not allowed for players to use, but lowers and sometimes kings use it when they are in danger or needed for other things," Emerson said as he turned his head in frustration.

"Carlos set you up." Cotton Anderson looked well-versed in terror. "Winter is Jewish and a child of prophecy. Carlos Diaz wanted Winter killed, but he did not know about the Red Horse organization built up in the Middle East to protect her. Winter was already immortal when she died in the pool with Pete. Carlos Diaz did not honor the incantations of that night. This is why Julia died."

"Carlos would have known Winter was already immortal," Madison claimed.

"No. He didn't. I promise." Anderson was serious.

"This will split the star network," said Oliver Material.

"Possibly," said Magellan.

"Why is this happening?" Pete asked.

"Some foundations have members like Al Thatch who no longer want to die themselves to obtain power," Anderson said. "Also," Anderson added, "they're racist and power hungry. Washington is slated to be a U.S. President: he's African American. And, Winter, you're Jewish."

Chapter Twenty-Two
Death

I, Elle, knocked on Winter's door. "My cameras don't work anymore. All bets are off. I'm going to continue my journey of documenting Winter's life, but I'll have to do it in person," I said as I walked into Winter's apartment. At this point I did not honor Carlos's request for me not to introduce myself to Winter as her historian.

"My name is Elle Magellan." I stretched out my hand to Winter Thompson, Pete Johnson, and Khalifa Mohammed. "I already know all three of you well. I am the group's historian. I, of course, have met Pete and Khalifa before now."

Two rocks lay on the ottoman.

The last candle flickered. It went out. Winter's windows were still closed to outside light to keep the warmth in the apartment.

"Someone is here," Winter said. "She said she could help us."

"Not kidding, Madison, I'm not cut out for this shit," Fouad said and turned. The men nervously laughed.

"We could use the dead and not Holy Guardian Angels to guide us," I said.

"Are they reliable?" Fouad asked.

"She says there are six of them," Winter explained.

"Good God," said Fouad.

"We need to make an oath between us to stay alive. I have risked it all for you all. Will you do the same for me?" Anderson asked the group.

"I will," Magellan and Washington said together.

"I will," the group said. The watches lit neither green nor red.

"We will just have to trust each other. Leave the watches on for as long as we can. We must give the appearance of compliance for as long as possible," Magellan said.

"No offense, Thomas, but that will not be long," I said. "To the dead I speak: Why is the game still afoot after Christmas midnight? Please tell Winter." Night was falling we could see through the apartment windows. No candles were still lit.

"They can also write on the wall they're telling me," Winter explained, "but I must be present. I will not be able to see it. Proceed, if you wish, I say to the dead."

The game is still on the ground because there is still a contract out on a seated king: Franklin Washington.

Pete read out loud for Winter as the words appeared.

"I don't understand," said Winter to the living group. "How can anyone die?"

"Even immortals have numbers. The higher-numbered player can kill the lower-numbered player. Anderson is higher than Washington in number. We are both in the thousands, though."

"Why, then, didn't I die squared at the pool when Carlos Diaz didn't honor the sacrifice?" Winter asked.

"Pete was lower than you when he killed you. You were already immortal on some level," Oliver Material explained. "When not in a poker round in an officially sanctioned casino, numbers count."

"If our initiates were not honored, how did Pete and I survive our first shot that night at the Bellagio?" Khalifa asked in horror.

"That is the right question," Magellan said. "You are both far enough along in the process, and you both must be very pure in heart."

The writing disappeared. New writing appeared: *Go to the cemetery. The dead will help you.*

Pete read out loud again.

"An oath is in order," I, Elle, said. "Thomas, administer it."

"We will not be bound by magic at this point. Carlos Diaz has cut us off," Magellan explained. "We will just have to trust our words."

All of the players and kings placed their hands in a circle and Winter was shown how to join hands with the person opposite her, thumbs locked and pinkies touching.

"Repeat after me," Magellan said. "I will not betray this company here at this moment." Everyone repeated Magellan.

Madison seemed to have recovered. He seemed resolute and angry that he had been betrayed by Carlos Diaz. "Let's go to the cemetery," Madison said.

"Hell, no," said Fouad. "I am not going up there again, particularly in the dark."

"Al Thatch has something to do with this," Winter decidedly said. "The dead are implicating him with their voices. The dead never lie, they are telling me. The dead are saying that unless we face Al Thatch at the cemetery, Osiris will win, which wouldn't be so bad except for the fact that Al Thatch currently has the most power in Osiris," Winter said as she started to show strength.

"Holy shit, I hate ghosts," Fouad responded. "That's true, Ms. Thompson – the dead never lie is a well-known saying in our world. What if they are lying? What if they are beholden to Carlos Diaz, and the cemetery is a trap?"

"We have to risk it. Not all of us, though. Six will go. Winter, do you dare? We need you to talk to the dead," Magellan asked.

"I dare."

"Elle, Washington, Madison, Fouad, Winter and I will go to the cemetery," said Magellan. "Pete, Khalifa, Emerson, Tweed, Material, and Anderson will stay here and try to run a séance to contact the dead independent of Winter."

"Yep. Going with Winter," Fouad said. "My God, we have become a creepy group of people."

"We need the dead," Magellan said. "Don't insult them."

"I won't be able to document your séance until we return."

"If we return," Fouad said. "That's my line."

Madison laughed. "We'll be fine."

"Famous last words."

In three cars, the group of six—I, Elle, Winter, Madison, Fouad, Magellan, and Washington--drove in the bright sunlight and through the heavily snowed streets to the cemetery.

Little rocks sat on top of all of the gravestones. "The stones represent prayers," I said. "Winter, stay close to me."

I am later writing this. I, of course, could not write as I watched at this point. So, one can know I lived. Still, what happened next was not happy for me or for any of us.

We headed to the dug-up part of the cemetery. Al Thatch stood there—new owner of the cemetery.

"Did the dead play us?" Fouad asked.

"Not possible," Washington said.

"I see you are at odds with Carlos Diaz," Al Thatch began. "As you know, I am with Osiris—although, most of my foundation does not agree with my belief we have died enough. It is time for innocents to die in our place. Does the rest of The Melville Foundation know the famed Magellan and Elle have defected from the star network?"

"Of course not," Winter's voice shook. "We are here on an errand. We know you are ever loyal to the Devil. We are too."

We were all startled to hear Winter address Al Thatch.

"Correct you are, Ms. Thompson." Al Thatch said. "I am ever loyal to Carlos Diaz. But, are you? Are you certain you are loyal? Produce your stone, Magellan."

"I do not have it," Thomas said to Al Thatch. "I have left it in the care of Richard Emerson." Unheard of.

"Why? Richard has his own stone. What goes on here?"

Al Thatch ominously walked around and through open graves to stand near Washington. The darkness seemed impenetrable.

"*Orcus!* Lend!" yelled Magellan. But he was too late.

"I've got your number, Franklin Washington," and Al Thatch shot him. Franklin Washington fell to the ground. Al Thatch turned and walked away to his car where his driver opened the door to him.

Franklin Washington breathed heavily. "I can see the dead. They are everywhere. The dead did not set us up. They are here." He died.

"Winter," Winter later told me, Elle, that a voice spoke in her ear. "It's me, Professor Washington. Run. I am now dead.

You all need to run."

"Run!" Winter yelled.

"Where?" Madison demanded.

"I don't know. I don't know."

"To the public street away from Thatch," Washington's voice sounded in her ear.

"To the far street!"

"We cannot leave Washington's body!" Thomas shouted.

"Leave it! Professor Washington says leave it!"

"Who?" Thomas asked.

We all started to run. "The dead are everywhere trying to create an illusion," Professor Washington whispered, Winter later told me. "There are hit contracts out on all your heads." From the construction site near the dug-up graves emerged men and women in black cloaks, masked. They moved toward the party.

"You just have to make it to the far street. Do not go to your cars on the left. Yell it!" Professor Washington's ghost darted up to Winter then seemed to drift away only to dart again. She couldn't see him, but she could hear him.

"Do not go to the cars. Make it to the far street, Washington says!"

"This is madness!" yelled Fouad.

The cloaked figures began to run.

What we knew but Winter did not is that the game cannot be afoot in the public street if at least twenty feet from a player's private property.

Winter stumbled in the snow. James Madison picked her up and helped her along. The group made it to he plowed street. We turned and watched the cloaked figures approach us at a dead run. I confess I prayed to Winter's Dark Angel's God that science worked.

The closest cloaked figure drew a gun and shot at Winter. It struck her, but she did not fall. I wondered in awe how high her number must be – also, the street plan worked. How long we were going to have to stand in the street was beyond me.

Sirens sounded in the air.

"Ah," said a dark figure. "We see science has bested us this time. Perhaps. Perhaps we'll wait."

The cloaked figures immediately turned and walked away toward the construction site.

"Walk to your cars. You are safe for now," Washington commanded Winter.

Winter repeated it.

Chapter Twenty-Three
Race

"No candles. No candles. We need Washington. I don't mind a ghost I know," Fouad was instructing Winter and me in his car.

Whenever two sides' kings officially dueled within a game in the star network, a race commenced. Some object must be found in order to win the race. "The race is on – maybe. Maybe," said Fouad. "Is anything the same, Elle, when we are now fighting Al Thatch and – wait for it – *the Devil*?"

"I imagine our independent wealth stays. But they'll come for it. They'll sue and attack from every angle to make us broke. This has happened in history before," I, Elle, said.

"And the *Devil* won, right? I mean. The *Devil* won. Right?" Fouad sounded incredulous he was in this circumstance at all. "How is it I was so stupid as to cross the Devil himself?"

"The Devil sometimes switches sides. Do not doubt we can prevail."

"What will happen to Washington's body?" Winter asked.

"Magellan will take care of it." I said.

"My God, I hate this," Fouad said. "Is Washington's ghost in the car? Ask him. car? Ask him, Winter, if the race is on."

"It's on, he said." Winter explained. "He is saying the object sought is a small seer stone extraordinaire. I don't know what this means."

"It means that when one group duels another and a stalemate is reached, what is called 'the race' begins," I, Elle, explained. "We are now in a race with Al Thatch as part of The Epictetus Dilemma Game. Duel races are always to find a magical object anywhere in the world. The small stone extraordinaire can provide sight and sound and other magical features I have never learned. I've never seen one. It is said there are only three in the world. A person who may have one would be like a U.S. President. They are very useful in war. Carlos Diaz is starting a war."

"Good God, Washington was slated to be a U.S. president," Fouad whispered it.

"Why is Al Thatch digging up a Jewish cemetery?" Winter asked.

"Make no mistake, Ms. Thompson," Fouad began, "Al Thatch is loyal to no human. He plays to win."

"Can we assume all dead will help us?" Winter asked.

"The dead are kind, albeit scary. Unlike demons who are just terrifying." Fouad said.

Chapter Twenty-Four
Séance Results

"Oh my God," Winter said. "What are demons?" Winter asked Fouad and me in the car.

"You apparently can't see them, Winter," I, Elle, said. "Carlos Diaz is the highest demon on the Earth. They are the most powerful beings save Diaz, and there are only thirteen. Together they form what is known as The Knights Templar. Many mythologies exist about the Knights Templar, but they are demons. Demons are not good, Winter. Everyone knows Carlos Diaz wants evil, but we are bound by contract. Early ancestors of ours wanted to be kings or nobility with wealth and made a deal with the devil. In exchange, they traded their descendants to Satan for all time. Some call it a curse. Some call it sound logic. Others call it magic. Many call it a blessing. Regardless, you are bound because of an earlier ancestor's decisions. Most of us try to be friends with Carlos. He is a part of our lives. But the Devil has a terrifying reputation for a reason. Demons are caretakers of Diaz's kingdom. If we face a demon, we are definitely fighting the devil himself. Carlos is only loyal to himself and his demons. He will turn on Al Thatch if Thatch loses this race. It is important that we win. You need to stay with us and help us with the dead's instructions. Do you understand, Winter?" I tried to sound as calm and kind as possible.

"I understand," Winter said.

Winter, Fouad, and I entered her building and walked to the second floor. When we opened the door to the living space, we found Anderson, Emerson, Tweed, Material, Pete and Khalifa standing in a circle.

"Washington is gone," I said as the men turned to look at us.

"We know," Emerson said, with tears running down his face. Partnerships were long-standing in Plato. On the ottoman between the men was a dead chicken. A towel covered the ottoman, and the chicken's neck was broken.

Winter looked distressed. "This is too much," she whispered.

"Where on Earth did you get a chicken?" Fouad, startled, had returned to his sarcastic self.

"Pete stole it from a farm just outside of Bloomington. Took him three minutes to Google the farm's location and an hour to get the chicken. We were startled ourselves." Emerson pulled himself together.

"I don't like the killing of animals," Winter said.

This is common, I'll add here. I am now writing on December 28, 2028, on a fifteen-hour flight in a plane to Dubai in the UAE where we were landing instead of in Abu Dhabi because the flights were sooner. Somehow, animal death was worse than apprentice or player deaths for everyone. Even immortals. Well, perhaps not everyone. Someone like Al Thatch would enjoy death of any kind.

The Epictetus Dilemma was extended to include the race. Right now, Al Thatch was considered in the lead. We were being fed information from Westfield players at St. Thomas who were risking their lives (squared) to help us. This wording perhaps sounds funny to someone not in our world. But to us, to lose one's life squared is to cease to exist before our time was up to make a difference, before one had a chance to fully love and live. Death squared meant the end of everything beautiful as far as we knew. To be. That was always the answer regardless of the game, be it The *Hamlet* Game, The Whitman Writings, or The Epictetus Dilemma. "To be" was always the answer. "To not be" was to die squared. To cease to exist, we thought. But Washington was still with us.

"Washington is with Winter," I explained. Emerson's mouth dropped.

"We have secured a death link," Anderson explained. "We can use Winter's stone to communicate with our tethered specter. He'll speak to us through the stone. His name, he writes on the wall, is Seth."

"That's great," I, Elle, said.

"Where are Magellan and Madison?" Tweed asked.

"They are trying to retrieve Washington's body. Thatch likely beat them to the body. Washington told Winter to tell us to leave the body and run. If we had not, we would have died squared," I explained.

"Al would have cleaned up the body before you reached as he is the one who killed him. Our specter said it was Thatch. We actually watched it happen."

Occasionally, a dead soul would have the title of specter. They could provide dreamlike visions (smoky, but clear enough) from objects chosen in a séance to tether the specter. Debates about whether or not tethered specters were ethical abounded. I explained this to Winter. "A tethered specter can provide visions. Some feel it is unholy to tether a specter. Dangerous even."

"I'll ask it," Winter said.

"Specters can only provide images and answers through

sight. They can hear like you," I, Elle, said.

"Specter tethered, do you wish to be set free?" Winter asked.

"No" scrolled in smoky capital letters across the wall.

Chapter Twenty-Five
Identification

"How do you all know all of this?" Winter wondered.

"We go to private prep schools, Ace," Pete said. "How are you doing? Did it scare you to see Franklin Washington die squared? The loss of Professor Washington is terrible." Pete was crying. Washington was his Henge Mage.

"I am not terrified of death anymore," Winter offered.

"Or ever," I, Elle, offered.

Just then, there was a knock on the door which revealed Magellan and Madison. "The body was gone. All traces of the body were gone by the time we got there," Madison offered as they entered. Madison was unusually shaken.

"Thank you for trying, Magellan and Madison." Emerson reached over to Magellan, and they hugged each other.

Fouad knew his role and tried to keep things light. "But it looks like Professor Emerson killed a chicken for your pleasure."

"Ah," said Madison. "How dark-mage like."

"Yes," Anderson said. "What darkness. We are in this race for good, and it will be as dark as it gets. We killed a chicken. Thatch will kill innocents at will to win to obtain information. I wonder if all seer stones are down – if Diaz shut them all off. If so, Thatch will sacrifice a human to obtain tethering. It's terrifying."

"I have only ever seen seer stones shut down once before. I confess it was all of them at once," Magellan offered. Thomas, my husband, seemed tired and a little broken. I went to him and put my arms around him. "I just wish we could have recovered his body."

"He's still here with us," Winter said.

"Tell us what to do, friend," Emerson sort of said to the sky in an effort to talk to Washington's ghost.

Winter said, "Washington's soul has said to arm ourselves to win. The seer stone is somewhere in the Middle East. Some say Abu Dhabi."

Pete looked up. "That's Khalifa's part of the world."

"The UAE will know about this. The U.S. star network is watched by Arabic nations at all times. They will know our civil war is coming to them," Khalifa said and sighed in frustration.

"I will book us all immediately," Anderson said. "We will fly out as soon as possible. In a couple of days if we can or sooner. I will book us in a hotel in Sharjah rather than in Abu Dhabi. We cannot just fly into the city we know the stone to exist in. Others will be watching us. Or Dubai. We can stay in Dubai."

"Does everyone have a current passport?" I asked.

"I don't," Winter said.

"Winter, find your identification cards, anything you have, a birth certificate too, if possible. We're going to get your passport immediately. It will look different than any other you have had before."

"I've never had a passport before," Winter offered.

"How did we miss this?" Anderson asked.

"Well," I began. "The star network is well known in the

United States and it is marked on your passport. I think it will still be honored as you are still in a game."

It was. It took myself and Winter six hours the next morning to obtain her passport. She had to be identified again and again so as to mark her passport as part of the star network. Some of the TSA workers seemed to support us. Some seemed to support Al Thatch. "Innocents die for quotas," was Thatch's motto. "We die ourselves for Diaz's quotas," was Magellan's motto. This was being said.

Chapter Twenty-Six
Flight

We flew from Minneapolis to O'Hare, and then we caught a flight to Dubai. From the Dubai airport, we caught a Careem taxi to the Hilton Creek Hotel. We stayed there for one night, and then we bought a Toyota SUV to take us to Abu Dhabi. We had word that Thatch beat us to Dubai by three or four hours, but that he was looking in the Dubai Mall at the shark tank for the stone.

The roads between Dubai and Abu Dhabi were insanely crowded and fast. When we reached Abu Dhabi, the tethered specter and Winter's dead guided us to the Abu Dhabi Louvre. We paid. We entered. We split up. Only Madison, Emerson, and Magellan came with us.

Lying beneath a painting of George Washington (we were surprised it was there) was a stone. It was the desired stone. We later heard Al Thatch's body was found in LaGuardia airport. Non players would not even notice it because of its powers.

Some say Cotton Anderson killed him. I think it was Carlos. The "lights" later didn't give up this information.

There was little debate that this act of winning the duel meant the three kids with hero's journeys still had much to do to secure peace in the Middle East in relation to stopping pro war advocates. Such would be a ten-year quest. What finding the small seer stone extraordinaire meant to the star network participants in the US was that my, Elle's team—Magellan's team—was going to be reestablished in Plato with our former titles in Carlos Diaz's good graces again. Winning was everything to Carlos. Dying ourselves instead of innocents dying to get the Devil's quotas had won one round.

Chapter Twenty-Seven
Game Not Over

When we received word Al Thatch was dead, our watches lit up. We had won, which meant we would be in good standing again with Carlos Diaz. Diaz hated weakness.

Madison was different though. He no longer felt the pride he had felt before. He was a changed man. He disliked Carlos Diaz, and one could feel he intended to fight. I returned to my location in Minneapolis. Camera views were restored to me. My Holy Guardian Angel visited again. Things moved forward as if we were never called traitors. Some called it the unwieldy nature of the game. "That's the way this crazy game goes," some said and chuckled in the way we used to. It had ceased to be that kind of funny for all of us. Jane was gone. Washington was gone. We felt the sting of our lack of properly mourning Julia's death.

We were declared the winners of the 2028 game The Epictetus Dilemma. We were paid accordingly. Al Thatch was determined to be the loser. Five Connect was sold. It was reported in the news that Al Thatch had a heart attack.

We now had an additional seer stone, one of three presidential stones – we learned from the stone's Holy Guardian Angel – as they were called. The stone was given to Pete and Khalifa to share by Carlos Diaz who said such a gift would help young people in a hero's path. "What powers do you have beyond teaching?" we asked the new stone's HGA. Stone information is called teaching.

The Holy Guardian Angel sent its angel image and then responded in sound and with visual words floating from the stone: "I can show you things past and future trajectories, but, beware: future trajectories are dangerous because they have not yet happened and can change."

Back at St. Thomas, Winter's apartment had become a sort-of meeting place for the St. Thomas Plato family. While the game had been declared over, a schism had formed in the star network between those who wanted to die themselves to reach Carlos Diaz's death quotas and those who wanted innocents to die for quotas using war and murder . Politics became fierce in the groups seemingly still at play. Plato Winter Winter Winter Winter Winter.

Chapter Twenty-Eight: The Great Conversation: January 12, 2029

Carlos Diaz had called everyone back in to Las Vegas as the game had gone over. "You shall all discuss death quotas and war in the Middle East before the whole of the star network as a family, as you call yourselves. You are the winners. You shall be celebrated."

Word had spread that Pete, Khalifa, and Winter were all on their hero's journey. Jealousy rather than horror abounded unfortunately for the three of them.

Emerson, Tweed, Madison, Fouad, Pete, Khalifa, and Winter were commanded to present a celebratory round highlighting the new game's title: The Sun in Abu Dhabi. As always, the question at play was to be or not to be. Anderson was to deal. Magellan was to fund the game as the game was one where bets were laid. The Sun in Abu Dhabi was a new kind of death poker.

Chapter Twenty-Nine
A New Kind of Poker as Recorded by the Bellagio Las Vegas

Anderson: Your Majesties, Alistair Tweed, Richard Emerson, James Madison, Oscar Fouad, Peter Johnson, Khalifa Abdul Mohammed, and Winter Thompson, this is a new kind of poker. Again, the goal is to be. To be or not to be? That is the question.

The company: To be. [green]

Anderson: That is correct. To be is the correct answer. This is a celebratory round for the winners of The Epictetus Dilemma. We have players who are not kings nor king starlets included here today. Lay your bets. Then I will deal the cards, which is new to 2029's game.

Madison: Is this a game of numbers? There are wagers? We lay our bets before we are dealt? [green]

Anderson: Before you are dealt. This is not a game of numbers. It is still of ideas.

Madison: I wager a million. [green]

Emerson: I call. [green]

The rest of the company called. [green unanimous]

Anderson dealt cards.

Emerson: These cards have philosophies on them. There are no face cards. [green]

Anderson: You've all been dealt your personal

philosophies about peace in the Middle East: ideas you have said at some point in your lives about peace in the Middle East. They are philosophy cards. Play each other. The truest speaker will take the wagers. Let's see if you all truly believe that to die yourselves is best and war is evil. Deal in. If you espouse an ideal not on your cards, you must account for the change from your cards or be shot. You are being held to your past words in print in this game–not just by what you clearly think now. Here is the initial idea deal: How do we bring about peace in the Middle East?

Diaz: Someone deal in.

Tweed: We must die ourselves. We should not perpetuate war in the Middle East to obtain death quotas. [green]

No one in St. Thomas disagreed with Tweed. No one dealt in.

Anderson: Khalifa, you find yourself in the game without a pistol. How does this make you feel?

Mohammed: I feel vulnerable. [green]

Anderson: Deal in anyway.

Mohammed: I think I can speak for my entire region. We do not want to die for anyone's greed. [green]

Anderson: Deal in Pete.

Johnson: I agree. War for death quotas is evil.[green]

Winter Winter Winter Winter Winter

End of transcript.

"Perhaps I have made a mistake by sending my youth into seated immortality too soon? They clearly do not have a taste for death or the game: this little debate is not heated." Carlos Diaz was his most congenial self. "You all can stop the game."

The audience quietly laughed and applauded.

I could tell Winter could not see Carlos. Mr. Diaz stood behind her. He placed his hands on the back of her chair.

"I'll stand here so my young immortal can hear me even if she cannot see me."

The audience applauded.

"This is the new kind of poker." Carlos swept his arm across the board. "And I am reinstating the youth into hero archetypes. They can handle it, but they will need to learn how to argue."

The fiercest parts of the crowd chuckled. Others looked on in horror but politely applauded.

"From now on, hero journeys will be started with players. Players will play immortals. Stones can be made from anything and everyone has a Holy Guardian Angel, no? The immortal great conversations have become a bit too boring for me of late The great conversation is called The Sun in Abu Dhabi next year. Prepare accordingly. This is the debate: Is Israel a sovereign nation and should it be? But, as always, the greatest question is to be or not to be?"

Winter looked in horror at Pete.

Applause filled the room.

She could hear but not see Carlos Diaz.

"Also," Carlos continued. "The Old Practices for voodoo will be reinstated starting tomorrow night in the desert. No clean-cut games this year. Show you have what it takes or not."

Applause.

Chapter Thirty
The Old Practices

Winter Thompson stood in the dark near a fire in the desert, the next night. Her hair was wild and adorned with a horned headdress. She held a voodoo doll of ancient style over the fire sacrificing herself rather than an innocent. It would not kill her; she was immortal. It was a new game. It was an old game.

The End.

Gabrielle Magellan.